ALONG A BURNING HIGHWAY

Along a Burning Highway

A Poetic And Story Filled Journey
Along That Jagged, Ragged Highway
Of The Heart Lost Deep Within The Joys
And Darkness Of The Mind

Written By:
Kerry L. Marzock

Along A Burning Highway

Published in the United States of America.

ISBN	Paperback:	978-1-959165-21-7
ISBN	eBook:	978-1-959165-22-4

ReadersMagnet, LLC
10620 Treena Street, Suite 230 | San Diego, California, 92131 USA
1.619. 354. 2643 | www.readersmagnet.com

Cover design by Ericka Obando
Interior design by Ched Celiz

Other books written
by Kerry L. Marzock:

Novels

• *Raven's Way*

• *Raven's Rage: Order of the Claw*

• *The Reptilian Factor*

* * *

Poetry

• *A Sea of Emotion*

FOREWORD

2010 was definitely a difficult test of endurance, battling through a very difficult period with an extremely sick husband, spending many months hobbling around on a painful right knee which I have recently gotten repaired under the skillful hands of a fantastic surgeon, and juggling all this with an intensely busy full time job (which I love), would test the strength of any person. Through it all, we've survived and life goes on with probably many more roadblocks and curves down this crooked path we all travel—aptly termed, "Along a Burning Highway".

Plans for completing several more novels this year did not come to pass, but this will occur for sure in 2011. As a result though, "Along a Burning Highway", is a depiction of life in general, definitely not viewed through rose colored glasses though. This book is a blend of poetry and short stories going from light to dark. Life is definitely a struggle from time to time and it's these rough passages that we ALL must face. Kind of makes this existence more than interesting.

Completing my two novels, **Raven's Way** and **Raven's Rage: Order of the Claw** was extremely gratifying to me, especially knowing that they were received well by Raven fans. The Raven Saga will definitely continue. Also possessing a true love of poetry my book "A Sea of Emotion", is a portrait of everyday life—a long journey of love, sadness, strong family ties, and loneliness as well. This new book takes that journey forward in a darkly poetic flow followed with some hard-hitting fiction.

I was a longtime resident of Philadelphia for 46 years and truly love that city. Sadly, during that time my husband Richard passed away. 'Love and miss you so much Richard'. Also, my wonderful and beautiful dog Rain crossed the Rainbow Bridge, but her memory lives on in my "Raven" series. Now currently living in Canton, Ohio, I am busy working on a new novel which I hope to have done by year end. Also, there was a third novel, **The Reptilian Factor**, published after **Raven's Rage: Order of the Claw**. Please take a moment to check out my website at: *www.kerrymarzock.com*. Also, you can always send an email to let me know what you thought of **Along A Burning Highway** to: *www.kmarzock@aol.com*

Acknowledgements

I think that every writer needs somebody who definitely believes in them. That person for me is Ken Cowle, my publisher at Soul Asylum, and my very, very good friend. Our weekly conversations help to bring both support and encouragement in good times and bad. Plus, we make each other laugh which is definitely needed quite often. And to all those werewolves, vampires, and assorted monsters out there who haunt my thoughts, giving me great ideas to keep writing about. Bring it on!

TABLE OF CONTENTS

SHORT STORIES

Dedication

I will always dedicate any books I'm fortunate enough in completing to my parents, Wanda and Eugene, who were an immense influence on my life who I loved beyond description. Sadly, both my parents have passed on but their spirits are with me always. To my awesome brother Rick who is a rock, a great husband and father, and is a very cool guy, even though he is a Steeler fan (GO EAGLES). Special dedication to my nephew Bret, who dedicated himself to getting in great shape, and then completed the Philadelphia marathon--so awesome and you are an inspiration to me. To all four of my very handsome nephews - Kirk, Bret, Ryan, and Nick - you make me very proud indeed. Lastly to my husband Richard, who had it very tough health-wise, over his last six years of life, but who let me know every day how much he loved and appreciated me. Very sadly, my Richard also passed away in April 2015. I miss him a lot. Oh, and I can't forget my loving dog Rain who never ceased to amaze me. Her wild and crazy spirit lives on in my 'Raven' novels. Love you Rain.

Along A Burning Highway

Can you hear the painful sobbing?
...deeply forlorn and weary worn beneath an angry sky
of chiseled gray, crimson teardrops fall in agony
drowning out these fractured thoughts of you
that cast a tortured spell upon this burning highway.

Can you smell the searing stench?
...sadly desolate and teary torn across this broken pavement,
through charcoal mist of leering gaze and veil of heartless scorn,
sunken, empty eyes forever sigh as harsh winds scream
in pleading shrieks a top this burning highway.

Can you feel the torrid scorching?
. . .while you kneel and pray on ragged thorns spread a top
this ragged tarmac, arms spread akimbo in silent supplication,
tragic hearts ablaze upon black silent wings of crows that soar
away with shattered dreams above
this burning highway.

Can you see the raging flames?
...amid lost nights and aimless days now shorn of kisses
once divine, a darkened fog of unheard prayers, anger so benign.
Day becomes night as night begets sorrow now adrift upon
this burning highway, charred hopes tossed upon
the pavement's edge. . .

Can you find the broken heart?
...a seared and dying rose lies scorned, forever lost and godforsaken,
still longing for that kiss, sweet lips of dreams and breathless sighs
now brushed a vivid, scarlet red ~~ enraged and a'flame~~
so frightened and alone amid icy, midnight bliss.

~~now forever lost along a burning highway~~

TART WINE, SWEET CHOCOLATE KISSES, AND A MELANCHOLY HEART

A bluish, silvery moon skims slowly upon waves of sadness,
glimmers of starlight clouding thoughts beneath a veil of salty tears,
this stark white canvas called life seems to be skillfully painted
with colorful bursts by the artistic brush strokes
of a surreal and thoughtful Salvador Dali.
The persistence of memory cries out for the tartness of wine
and the sweetness of chocolate kisses to assuage this
broken heart, forever colored melancholy!

Willowing quiet breezes swept from fading love combine
with the intoxication of Chablis and the enchanting
aroma of sweet Hershey kisses. Tis' at least a
precious moment of sweet reciprocity.
Open and painful wounds from heartbreak
temporarily mended by a short, cool sip of wine
and a sweet chocolate kiss within a forlorn and aching
heart that longingly yearns for sensuality.

MISSING YOU

It's been such a long time since I held you,
remembering how the electricity raced through my arms
that I often wonder if it was all just a distant memory.
A mirrored reflection within a crystal cool,
mountain pool that shimmers and ripples,
emerging into sharp focus briefly,
then quickly losing shape, hauntingly teasing urgent
desire and longing before sadly evaporating
forever amid the glimmering haze of love.

Yet even still, each time I allow your name to caress
the frayed edges of my mind I feel like a white rose
a' bloom in all its pure, summery glory.
Covered by the softness of night, my heart bursts
like a super nova of creamy vanilla and golden wheat
softly brushing my senses with a thirst, a rabid hunger
to become lost within your warm embrace,
my thoughts crying out how much I've missed you
locked inside these lonely nights and silent days.

IT HURTS SO MUCH TO LOVE YOU

Falling in love with you was the easy part,
your magical personality, that cool but silent grace.
The sheer tenderness of your sweet and soothing voice
that reached deep within to gently massage this frantic heart.
Anxious fingertips softly traced the contours of your face,
teardrops breaking free at just the frightening notion
we could sadly ever painfully drift apart.

It hurts so much to love you that at night,
when urgent loneliness is so pervasive,
all that's left is to cry myself to sleep.

It's so easy to become entangled inside a tricky web of love,
while frantically plunging off a terrifying precipice
to tumble forever deeper from a ragged edge
of shattered pain above, reeling head over heels
toward an unknown rocky shore, captured securely
in thoughts of love rarely ever touched before,
wondering if true love will again grace this open door?

It hurts so much to want you
when you're not around that I can't help
but let this heart cry out, so impossible not to weep.

You know when a heart is torn and fragile, so ever breakable
~ spinning, lost and whirling ~ no longer in control.
Yet that knowledge still makes loving you undeniable,
forever worth the painful risk for even the slightest moment
of no longer having that special thrill of holding
you so tight, feeling two hearts beat as one
in true alignment deep into the night.

It hurts so much to need you
when times get tough, days of loneliness utter hell,
that it's the memories and tenderness one yearned to keep.

To lie nestled and safe within a deep and warm embrace,
amid love's pure rapture ~ oh ~ be still the night.
Yet, I've come to realize that deep within this silent heart,
echoes of love now such a long and whispered sigh,
was sadly dry, forlornly lost before you came.
Falling in love with you then was just the start,
my life enriched forever and never again to be the same.

WHEN THE NIGHTTIME HURTS

The emptiness of the bedroom still whispers
your name through a thin, gauzy framework
of loneliness. Your scent still so overwhelming.
tickling the edges of desire, teasing the texture
of yearning like how these fingertips many times
traced a path down those sweet valleys of pure pleasure.
How the frantic nighttime still hurts without
the tender sound of our laughter
and the soft expectancy of your exploring hands
upon this anxious, urgent skin.
The darkness drapes over me like a leaden blanket,
so utterly heavy and compressing,
suffocating while this heart beats madly~
pounding insanely for ONLY you

~now gone~

the chimes of the clock ringing
hour upon lonely hour in
unison with the painful
echoing of this weary heart ...
I do know where you are,
~ waiting ~ but, for how long?
Weeks and months march by like
the stomping of beleaguered soldiers,
wounds trying to heal, loneliness
and guilt like twisted sisters
chained tightly together.
Yet still, when bloodshot eyes
finally close to the burning
of forsaken dreams I see
your face ~ and that's
when the nighttime
really hurts.

LET IT NEVER END

* ~ * ~ * ~ *

Pure night of bliss
~ a gentle kiss ~
sweet scent of you
upon these crimson lips.

* ~ *

Warm wistful sighs
~ soft, midnight eyes ~
I call you forth to
seek these anxious hips.

* ~ *

Come to me now
~ as silence wanes ~
Oh, let me bow
o'er lover's smooth refrain.

* ~ *

Ever lost in hot embrace
~ our passion screams ~
a smile now etched upon your face,
adrift on starlit dreams.

* ~ *

Soft satin thoughts
~ hot desires quenched ~
'twas you I sought.
Please let it never end.

* ~ * ~ *

Our Perfect Place

Sometimes we go there,
to a very special place where thoughts
of pain and being alone are all but forgotten,
at least for a minute, perchance a longer time.
Closing my eyes I can hear your breathing,
strong and secure, so sure in the love we share.
A smooth and gentle whisper lying upon my ears
like lonely waves lapping against that distant shoreline
we once walked barefoot upon, the crush of warm sand
caught between our toes...fingers tightly interlaced...
so damn afraid to let go...to even open our eyes.

But then...the barest of words...
I love you
causes my heart to stop...then beat fast...
to quickly stutter...yes, to flutter once again.
My God...
dare I reach out to see if this is real,
not perhaps just a dream, that the warmth I feel
beside me is from your body, the skin I always yearn to touch.
Eyes tightly shut, I desire nothing more than to enjoy
the sensual aroma of being so near to you,
the beautiful, lyrical notes of a magical harpist
that special key to unlock this lonely heart,
the shaded window to my soul.

In the bedroom now...
a gently running brook just outside our window,
soft and gentle breezes blowing warmly...
gauzy, white curtains fluttering gracefully like butterfly wings,
a poetic dance of love and deepest desire.
It's still within the quiet darkness of early morning,
the breath of dawn but a distant, far off thought,

never wishing this cherished moment to end.
Light from a full moon dresses our feet in silver frost...
cool sheets caress our backs...then a gentle kiss...
the sweet taste that lingers upon our lips...
a sensual tingle down my spine I pray never to be lost,
held tightly within your warm and protective arms
knowing that you'll forever be near.

You reach for me...
I smile...
fingers placed where loving prints were so often left before.
We mold our bodies as one like interlocking pieces
of a puzzle we worked so hard putting together.
Your scent intoxicating like the finest of aged wines,
my head dizzy as your hands run softly over the heart strings
you often played with such finesse, the dexterity
used to propel me up the mountain and then
ever so gently carrying me back down.

It is the perfect place,
one I hope to never, ever leave,
never to let go of, to stay locked within these walls
just knowing that you're here,
that you'll always stay beside me.
Your anxious fingertips roaming...caressing...arousing...
opening wide these closed rooms within my soul.
Something wet now trickles down upon my cheek,
a lonely teardrop fallen in hopes that when I open these eyes
I'll still see your smile, fully aware you are truly there.

This is a very special place...our perfect place...
so my sweet love, come travel with me now,
perhaps upon those exquisite wings of monarch butterflies,
to places we always yearned to spend together,
no matter whether my eyes are open or remain closed,
just reach out to hold my hand
and please...please...
never let go.

A TASTE SO BITTERSWEET

It rolls across my tongue,
such a vile, acrid taste of bittersweet acrimony.
Those final words so sharp, slicing across
this wasteland that is now my withered heart, seared
like hot, blowing sands from stifling desert winds.
This bittersweet taste seeps
into tortured thoughts, all desire
crushed to dust, dreams now splayed
apart as stretching sinew screams.
This wretched taste of loss
so consuming that it rips away
the fabric of who I am, prayers I
once so desperately held onto now lost,
the hope of smiles and happiness
a' float on waves of deepest despair.
Your words have sent this ship a' sail
to who knows where?

Down~down~reeling

into a dark, lonely chasm to which all lost souls fall,
burnt ashes of tortured hearts lying tearfully,
forever piled upon one another, a horrifying
funeral pyre where dreams have died away.
I can hear the children of the night singing
their song of farewell, your words echoing
within my ears to forever last a lifetime.
This acerbic taste of bittersweet farewell
to lie painfully upon my bed of silence,
blackened ashes of a lost heart
blowing through darkened clouds,
along lonely streets, beneath
moonless nights and starless skies,
to now float forever upon a sea
of bittersweet existence.

BE STILL THE NIGHT

Darkness drapes me like sheer silk,
the cooling smoothness feeling like your
comfortable fingertips on a chilly December night.
I can still feel your breath against my lips.
Smiling, my mouth opens just a little,
awaiting your urgent exploration …

~ ~ ah, there it is ~ ~

that incredible taste of you like a burst
of pure, ripe sweetness from crisp grapes
on a sultry, sunny afternoon.
Your hand tenderly cradles my head, searching fingers
lost within my dark auburn hair, anxious lips caressing mine.

Soft breezes from the open window brushes against my breasts.
or be that your gentle touch? With my eyes closed
it truly doesn't matter ~~ it just feels so heavenly.
Blending smoothly into your arms I feel safe,
secure, so ever cherished, like your sun
rises and sets within these soft, brown eyes.

The haunting sound of a wayward owl from afar ~
or be that a moan arising passionately from my throat?
Moving closer ~ tighter ~ like the firm fit
of leather encasing my burning skin now set a' fire.
Silken moonbeams blanket us in a soothing glow
while glittering stars dance amidst the delight of romance.

~~ Oh sweet Eros, be still the night~~

EMPTINESS CRIES

Roses dying,
pinks of softness
fade away.

Lonely breezes sighing,
somber grays of darkness
lie upon yesterday.

Happiness now flying
on wings of blue Tomorrow's,
smiles no longer shining.

Empty tears of sorrow
pine again for loving days,
such sweet desires rising.

Thoughts of you in purple haze,
hearts so once defining,
have I lost you on the 'morrow?

Fading dreams of buttered skies
drift away on timeless rhyming,
your name at rest upon these lips.

Our love mirrored images in my eyes
while roses die and fade away.
as emptiness now cries.

CAN YOU HEAR THE WHISPER?

Listen closely to the throaty trill
of warm and sultry summer days, whistling
through thin gauzy curtains of longing.
Oh sweet scarlet tanager, vibrant
reddish flame of spring ~ your voice
is but the mist from softly rolling seas~

chick-bree ~ whoosh ~ chick-bree~

a warm breeze from summer's sigh
whispers gently against my tingling skin.
The padding sound of urgent feet
quickly crossing a cool, hardwood floor,
eyes shut tightly, aching for your tender touch
~ waiting ~ pining ~ longing ~
can you hear the whisper of seeking fingers
gently running the length of thighs
and anxious rise of breasts?

Chick-bree ~ ahhhhhhh ~ chick-bree ~

vibrant skin a' blaze with a song of crackling
logs nestled within a toasty fireplace.
Tenderly, a silky wisp of luscious lips
take flight on midnight's breath,
the twinkling in our eyes
all the starlight that we need.

Chick-bree ~ mmmmm ~ chick-bree ~

Can you hear the urgent whisper of "I love thee?"

Author's note: Chick-bree is the sound made by the scarlet tanager.

THE EARLY MORNING RAIN

I love to sit surrounded amid the reflective silence
upon the front porch while a softly falling rain
spreads mist within the early morning dawn.
It tenderly caresses the awakening
desires of a new day's virginity.

Sitting quietly with my dog Rain resting at my feet
I smiled, gazing wistfully towards a gunmetal gray sky.
A gentle mist from a cleansing shower glistened sensually
upon my skin, so thin it often resembled a
curtain of sheer, gossamer silkiness.

It's that somber, thoughtful time of moodiness
between disappearing darkness and the shadowy
grays of a burgeoning storm, not allowing the sun
to so much as crack the thick, weathered
blanket of a pensive and brooding dawn.

A gentle breeze that can smoothly caress your face like
a lover's tender fingertips, blows your
hair quietly against relaxed shoulders, permitting you
to smell the cool fresh scent of recently mowed grass
wafting silently upon a layer of pristine mist.

You can hear the dramatic drumbeat of a steady soothing
waterfall of early morning rain like the warning hiss
of a very wary serpent, only broken now and then
by the whoosh of angry, slippery tires
from the cars of half asleep, complacent drivers.

The glittering rain is a mirrored reflection of our lives,
sometimes gentle and comforting, so calmly reassuring and pure.
Yet often baffling and wondering lost in confusion,
but always steady and secretly sure of nothing.
Closing my eyes, I so enjoy the early morning rain!

MELANCHOLY THOUGHTS ON A FALL DAY

Dried and brittle leaves fluttered down
in a zany race to see which one would be first to kiss the ground,
spreading wide a gorgeous, vibrant gown of fall colors.
In such a painful, melancholy way, it resembled
these hollow tears I've shed for you now
that you are no longer around.

Flashes from a bright, scintillating sun
sliced imploringly through partially nude trees,
welcoming warmth unable to break apart
a stubborn, imposing phalanx of unheard pleas.
Passing cars whip up the tiny red and yellow
pieces of fall into questioning tornadoes.

Suddenly, the wind roared like an angry lion,
scattering a skirt of frightened, brownish-orange leaves
like a terrified herd of stampeding bison crossing a raging river.
A strong, forceful gale brushed against my shuttered eyes to
try and wash away such feelings of haunting melancholy.
Sadly, this cleansing wind was simply temporary.

Smiling at two dogs as they romped and played
happily amidst this lush, fall harvest of leaves,
comically chasing a soccer ball and then each other.
I wondered if perchance their innocence would possibly
rub off to brush this vast emptiness with a stroke of romance?
Leaves fell painting another melancholy tapestry of a fall day.

CROSSROADS OF THE HEART

Kneeling in the dust of time,
opening an old suitcase of memories,
listening to those harried voices saying~~
you can't do this. . .going that
way is not safe. . .society frowns
upon being different. . .be very careful
of traps and roads leading toward
danger. . .watch out for narrow
minded people who would
rather destroy than extend
a helpful hand, sharp fingers
more like clawed paws of
the reaper with grim
eyes and a leering
smile, broken teeth clattering madly ~ ~ ~

damn ~ always standing in the middle
of yet another four-way crossroads. . .
feeling the frantic winds of time
angrily buffeting this body from all directions,
hearing the melodic warbling of a
nearby stream singing ~ GO EAST ~ but. . .

that road seems so dark and stormy, forever
tired of always being knocked down upon
bloody knees. A passing goose overhead
honks out ~ GO SOUTH~ but. . .

the blistering heat of withered days
are not nearly to my liking.
In the troubled sky a jet black raven,
the one that has graced my dreams
in a lifetime of Tomorrow's, caws out
~ GO NORTH ~ that is where your

angel with the golden hand toils, he who holds
the magical key to change a life of textures,
sweet precious pill to swallow and thus disappear
to emerge upon the other side of metamorphose,
but...nothing is ever as easy as it seems to be ~
the key clutched tightly as the snap from lock
unclasped, echoing loudly~ that old friend,
the mirror ~ ~ wavering ~ ~ shimmering ~ stepping
anxiously through to yet another fractured pathway.
A lifetime of crossroads forever traveled, always
more to come ~ a glow spread upon distant horizon ~
rolling waves from a turbulent sea of emotion sailed
upon for so long... dark feathers lying upon a
broken highway~ the raven's way ~
~ GO WEST~ it screamed,

that's where love and happiness dwell.
Stepping forward ~ toward...
gazing down at chains strapped to ankles,
frantically searching for one more key
to release this wayward traveler
to start walking down just one more lonely road,
footsteps crunching upon one more solitary
highway, tightly clutching this ancient
suitcase of swirling memories,
reaching out for you. . .behind
the shadows of simply one more
empty crossroads.

BEYOND TOMORROW

Darkness descends
upon these bleakest days,
an endless parade of memories
that robs me of what light yet still remains,
your smile of radiance, those eyes
that glittered gaily in the sun whenever you
gazed at only me.

Your untimely death a tragedy
I will never understand, walking aimlessly
along the water's edge, my hand so
empty, yet still the feel of your fingers
caress my palm, the lapping waves whispering
your name, salty tears descending down to
lips—the kiss that o'er remains.

I linger beside your graveside, longer days
and lonely nights that forever have no meaning,
no purpose, other than to tell you over and over
how much I yearn to be together once again.
There are always those who state that life
goes on, that all will be as once it was,
but loving you is all I am.

Now there is no day, or night, just a deep
longing that seems to never end ~ and so ~
I close my eyes to see your smiling face,
arms and hands outstretched to touch the reaching
fingertips of mine, heartbeat fading to a deathly silence.
Though soft breath of here and now may be gone,
the grace of love is ours forever.

HEART IN A BOTTLE

~~~ Floating ~~ floating ~~
~~~ Aimlessly adrift ~~~
~~~ UP and down ~~~ undulating ~~~
sensing the softness of you against my skin.
Nothing but a broken heart encased within a lonely bottle,
an empty prison made of clear, shiny glass.
Staring back, I can see the somber, distant shoreline
so very far away, a rippling golden ribbon of sand,
fading smaller, growing dimmer.
I think I see you holding up your hand,
smiling through shallow tears, waving good-bye.

I glance up to see a huge wave come crashing down.
carrying me under, propelling me forever deeper
into a dark blue abyss of loneliness and misery.
Spinning ~~~ sinking ~~~ drowning in a sea of tears
Breathe, damn it. Breathe! Reach up!
Don't want to ...Can't ...
WON'T...
Allowing the deadly silence, the glittering blue water
to take me where a heart can never break again.
This bottle now my lonely resting place inside
A floating cemetery, a sea of memories without end.
Suddenly bobbing recklessly upon the glassy surface,
blue water now smoother, like mirrored glass.
I see your fading face smiling back at me,
haunting every single thought, whispering something.
The harsh sun glaring down as I sail away,
lost to who knows where, but then who really cares!
A brilliant white seagull dives down,
pecking away at what's inside this glass cell,
fractured heart barely beating, shattered into pieces,
simply decaying carrion for hungry, beady eyes.
~~~

Angrily, the bitter bird screeches and flies away.

Quiet now, nary a sound,
afloat on these silent waves of sighs.
So many words left unspoken as I drift in sorrow,
endlessly for days and weeks, for month upon month,
wondering if I'll ever taste your love again.
This bottled prison suffocating, strangling all desires to
continue on, too weak to care, too tired to fight.
I always wondered if you could die from a broken heart.
I know now the answer is simply yes.
Though I'll always love you, I cling
to the hope there will be another tomorrow.

IN A DESPERATE HEARTBEAT

Slowly opening my eyes, feeling so all alone,
never felt this lost before, unable to feel the floor.
This lonely house with empty sighs containing
shattered dreams of love long gone.
'Cause you won't be back in my life anymore.
We had a dream, a love that seemed so strong.
Feelings fade away sometimes,
strained emotions turned all wrong.
Came the day when you pulled back,
confusing words all tangled in between.
But I wonder if perchance
I'll ever see your smile again.

In a desperate heartbeat~~
my voice cries out your name.
Within a desperate heartbeat~~
my life shall never be the same.
Inside a desperate heartbeat~~
think back on what we overcame.
In a desperate heartbeat ~~
we both should share the blame.

Crying amid the silence, no longer lost within your spell.
Sometimes I fear the insanity, too often it hurts like hell.
When you find that special someone, better hope that love
Prevails or the devil may be knocking loudly at your door.

In a desperate heartbeat ~~
a silent voice calls out your name.
Inside a desperate heartbeat ~~
I shall never feel the same.
Within a desperate heartbeat~~
it doesn't matter who's to blame.
For everything now has changed ~~

in just a desperate heartbeat.
All these never ending days
overflowing with raging sorrows.
Desperately longing for a way
we can bring back our lost Tomorrow's.
For if you love someone today
hold them closely to your heart.
For yesterday they're here,
but in the morning they may be gone.

Held your sweater against my cheek,
closed my eyes and saw your smile.
Sweet memories I will always keep
brings you near for just a while.
Upon the sheets I still see your mark,
echoes of your breath within the dark.
This shattered heart cries against the night
to let us try again, keep reaching for the light.

I still possess this deep desire for you
so why can't you hear my call?
All my yesterdays now a stormy blue,
for seems we had no time at all.
Somewhere, someplace you're near,
I can't let your love disappear.
But until then ~ I'll always believe.
Forever believe—in the love we weave.

In a desperate heartbeat~~
my voice cries out your name.
Inside a desperate heartbeat~~
I shall never be the same.
Within a desperate heartbeat~~
if I need to then I will take the blame.
For everything has changed,
in this final desperate heartbeat~~

TEARDROPS, WHISKEY AND HEARTACHE

Just another empty shot glass and another silent tear.

Sometimes...
the only thing left to say is just a sad good-bye,
to watch you through these teardrops
as you sadly drive away.
Wondering where love went so wrong.
praying that you'd stop and maybe turn around
to simply smile and say, "I love you,"
like so many times before.

Sometimes...
the hiss of dried leaves whisper a song of memories
with no time left to sit and cry.
Angry words and feelings now crushed
as you harshly slammed the bedroom door.
Let this scathing whiskey burn away these sorrows
to feel the scalding taste of bitterness
try and wash away the pain.

Sometimes...
Momma used to say that just a shot or two of whiskey
could only last a minute, but heartache may never fade away.
Yet our memories cry for distant yesterdays
through misspent hopes of lost Tomorrow's.
Oh dear Momma, you were wrong I guess
'cause teardrops, whiskey and heartache
are all there is today.

Sometimes...
the only thing left to do
is simply smile and walk away.

TATTERED SHOES

While rummaging through a quiet, sleepless attic,
alone with thoughts inside this misspent night,
she gazed wistfully at boxes beneath a sheet of dust,
to lie unpacked, yet sealed so tight.
Her fingers shook as she opened one, and there
lying atop that lonely pile of memories
a single, tattered shoe did rest.
Sitting gently back, she softly erased a lonely tear
as she remembered some happy days
and held this shoe against her beating breast.

She wondered, whatever had possessed her
to spare a tattered shoe like this.
After all, it should have been discarded
with all her other distant memories.
Now it rested softly upon a trembling hand
as her mind spun backwards through the years.
Like a broken time capsule now ajar
allowed her time to reminisce.

She remembered buying this very pair of shoes
as they once gracefully held her feet.
A golden glass of wine so sweet,
brushed against a warm and tender smile.
A star-filled night with two hearts dancing,
she gently closed her eyes and saw his handsome face.
Her arms caressed the moon with grace
as she floated on dreams of pure romancing.

Months passed by before she wore these shoes again.
Gay ribbons, pink and blue, atop tiny gifts
amidst a baby shower with all her loving friends.
Sometimes later they carried her to a nervous class reunion.
She thought it was the tenth, or at the very least, what she recalled
Then months later to a school and a teacher's open house.
She remembered the haunting echoes of laughing children
as they drifted down those empty halls.

Like brilliant, falling leaves on a crisp, autumn day
all these memories came flooding back to her.
Melancholy thoughts long stored away,
caressing her mind like the healing aroma of chamomile tea.
She touched those tattered shoes to her lips
and thanked them for dreams she had long forgot.
A lonely teardrop ran down her cheek,
sadly tracing a life now for naught.
Sweet times kissing her like the taste of honeydew
as she remembered the many miles that she had walked
inside these old and tattered shoes.

A LIFETIME OF Tomorrow's

Slowly, painfully the memories cascade down,
like a wall of bricks sadly one atop the other
in a fragile and relaxed frown
of somber and forgotten headstones,
a lifetime of lost Tomorrow's.

One after another, like scarlet rose petals
that promise sweet smiles of
happiness in the dawning years,
silent prayers and dreams coast ever
painfully on an overcrowded highway of tears.

Craving that even one tomorrow will be
more fragrant than yesterdays.
So tired of sobbing over what may have been,
while reaching out to discover
passing dreams of tenderness in loving ways.

Praying that thoughts of happiness will at last
overshadow the nightmares of dark sorrow.
Yearning that the rose of promise will
magically appear on a rainbow
of embraces, saying a final farewell to a
lifetime of longed for Tomorrow's!

RAINDROPS AND HEARTACHE

Ashen grayness of the day
brushed her face with a shade
of weathered alabaster,
raindrops drumming atop
a battered and blue umbrella.
Not from the raging storm,
but rather a haunting farewell
to love thus spurned.

! ! ! ! !

Teardrops marched ever sadly
down a reddened cheek
to kiss sweet memories
she once lovingly caressed,
now madly swept
like rain drenched leaves
upon darkened streets.
Through the loneliness...she wept.

! ! ! ! !
Daddy wasn't there
to kiss away her empty tears,
protect her from the fears
of touching heartache once again.
Alone to face rejection
like the silent chambers
of an empty gun,
tears now seared her face
to form scars
now painfully etched,
creating deep and painful wounds
from freshly fallen
raindrops and heartache.
!!!
!!
!

STARING DEATH IN THE EYE

The evening didn't quite start out to be so
totally doomed and screwed up,
even though nagging, somber thoughts of
lonely desperation had continued
to echo madly against the sad persistence
of such a young and fractured existence.

However, as the evening wore on ...

depression reached out with evil,
greedy fingers to hungrily strangle
an already splintered life.
The sweet medicine of long island iced teas failed
to give courage to a person who had forever
silently cried out loudly for self-expression.

It was simply time to say good-bye...

amid ghostly steam from a shower of angry tears
completely clouding the mirror of her life.
Encased in a metal casket, the vehicle was a deadly weapon
careening madly down a long, dark, deserted country road,
the demon sneering wickedly with a welcoming evil grin
saying it was time to cease a life of endless trying!

With eyes closed, she smiled and heard ...

metal grinding, tires screeching,
glass shattering, poles and trees exploding.
Suddenly slamming painfully at Death's bloody door,
the mouth of Hell creaked open into that darkness of nevermore.
Extending trembling arms in thankful gratitude the troubled
young woman realized there was nothing left worth living for.

Then ...a sweet, angelic voice whispered in my mind ...

"It's not yet time for you to die for
there is another person you need to set free!"

Angry and forlorn, bloody and racked with physical pain,
consumed with emotional turmoil raging and aflame,
she realized that maybe Hell was this place called Earth.
That it was here where Satan's army of demons reigned,
creating obstacles and trials to either fail or overcome.
She had spoken to angels and danced with the Devil.

What in God's name was left to be done?

Only time would tell, but at least there was a new chance.

THE FOG

It's such an ominously surreal world,
lost within this mysterious fog.
I waded through hungry tendrils a' swirl around
a sense of apprehension and a very curious dog.

~ ~ ~ ~ ~

Insanely creepy,
eerily strange,
darkly alien,
a landscape for the deranged.

~ ~ ~ ~ ~

Stagnant air so deathly disturbing
that I could hear whispers from arousing flowers
mingle with the anxious chirping
of yawning, early-morning browsers.

~ ~ ~ ~ ~

Lost amid this realm of sin,
a shroud of pallid gray
tickles my skin,
beseeching arrival of a burgeoning day.

~ ~ ~ ~ ~

Frightened eyes
peer into a dense curtain
of insistent and breathless sighs,
these anguished thoughts of you uncertain.

~ ~ ~ ~ ~

An imperious, arrogant owl hoots alone.
I swear it called out your name.
Or maybe not ~ just a painful moan,
a morning song of beckoning rain.

~ ~ ~ ~ ~

As we walked, the fog lifted its gaze
through glistening leaves towards the sun.
This alien terrain now awash in a golden haze,
eyes staring through tears for that special someone.

DANCING WITH THE DEVIL

Often the devil comes wearing different masks so be prepared to share
the waltz of death. For when a horrid voice whispers "last dance"
it could well in fact be true, no matter how painful it may be.

Harsh, accusing neon lights
reflect garishly off smut-stained windows,
just another Big Apple, midnight city rainbow.
A kaleidoscope of pulsing signs screaming out in sin.

"X-RATED MOVIES, LIVE PEEP SHOWS"
"FORTUNE TELLER OPEN 24 HOURS"
"BREAKFAST AFTER MIDNIGHT"
"PRIVATE ROOMS—$10.00"

A flashing, nearly empty, pink and green champagne glass
leans precariously against an out-of-place, lonely
palm tree, its barren leaves not moving a hair
within this chilly, early May, forlorn air.
Sadly, it seems to be just another grim
and haunting, New York City nightmare.

~ ~ ~ ~ ~ ~ ~

The young woman lay sprawled across an empty floor
comprised of large and cold, black and white tiles.
A slowly spreading pool of dark crimson
encircled a mass of long, lush, auburn hair that
softly framed her battered, but pretty face.
Ragged pieces of tattered silk and lace
partially covered up her nude exterior,
finally afloat for at least awhile
in an oasis free from painful torment.

It was simply a date with kismet.
Nothing more than a single innocent hello,
lost within one more boring night of vacant smiles.
Merely a few more angry drinks lined in a row
much like a parade of half-drunken soldiers
staggering madly down a tear-stained bar.
She wondered if her lost, empty life
could become much worse.
Misty-eyed, she traced a lonely
question mark upon a sweaty
glass of Jack Daniels.

"So, would you like to get out of here?"
She gazed up at this stranger with sandy brown hair
and what appeared to be a friendly smile.
Mmmm, he did have those baby-blue, bedroom eyes.
She touched his cheek and sighed,
"Sure honey, you look safe enough to me."
Passing through the austere, black and red doorway
she winked at her roommate, holding up
and shaking their apartment key.

* * * * * *

An overturned, broken lamp
lay crumpled against a faded blue wall,
still casting a God-forsaken, haunting glow
across a cracked, dingy white ceiling.
It writhed painfully, as if a gruesome Danse Macabre
angrily kissed the rumpled, blood-stained sheets.
A solitary ceiling fan groaned a steady
mantra within her fading threads of
unsteady consciousness.

Realizing death might be near, she was aware
that to dance with the Devil was something
to fear. But, who knew the beast could
ever have such sweet, baby-blues?

A solitary sigh
escaped her broken lips.
She had no cause to be alarmed
for in a way she welcomed death,
a fitting epilogue to a life so unfulfilled.
The sad disappointment would be to simply die
alone lying upon this cold and barren floor,
her stark white nudity awash beneath a flashing
neon dress, peacefully waiting to whisper
a final farewell with what breath remained
to a life that seemed to hold no promise.

* * * * * *

"Oh ...my ... God ..." came the voice of an angel
breaking through the gauzy veil of blood-stained mist.
The stark garishness from a judgmental light bulb
tried to slice through a narrow slit in one eye
as she attempted to crack a crooked smile.
With just the barest hint of a whisper, she asked
"What ... took you ...so long?"
This young woman had in fact fought desperately
to remain awake, and thus, to stay alive.
At last, she succumbed to the welcoming darkness,
her midnight dance with the devil just one more
painful step along Hell's darkened highway.

SHATTERED

shattered pieces
fallen snow
frozen teardrops
please let me go ~

broken mirror
pieces splayed
eyes downcast
the end of days ~ ~

fractured heart
burning sun
hands outstretched
our love now done ~ ~ ~

splintered dreams
lonely nights
darkness here
there's no more light ~ ~ ~ ~

broken pictures
fractured glass
splintered hopes
life shattered at last ~ ~ ~ ~ ~

THOUGHTS OF A BROKEN POET

Romantic words once upon a time spoke easily
from this heart, sweet dreams clutched tightly
within these anxious fingertips. They can still feel
the silkiness of your skin, a sweet softness of lips,
the lush cascade of hair against an urgent cheek.

I thought of you this morning while the early rays
of sunshine tried to wash my nightmares away.
Memories are all that remain, grasping frantically
before they disappear completely, hot and lonely
tears now all that saturate each hopeless day.

In the shower, scalding water tore at my heart,
thick steam clouding my eyes, blurring what
visions I still retained of us together. I thought of you
while the burning water turned my skin a bright
pink, then fiery red like the harsh words that final night.

Anxious thoughts of you tumble down upon me
like hail from a torrential hailstorm. But still...my
heart cries out for you. Why is that and will there ever
be an end to this flow of tears that wildly crashes against
a fractured sky now forever devoid of love and romance?

Reaching out, I quietly grasp this pen, words of passion
no longer falling easily from my quiet lips, the twinkle
in these brown eyes replaced by loneliness and longing.
I thought of you so much throughout these many days
that I wondered what a broken poet writes about…

nothing…
abject silence...
utter emptiness...

JUST THIS SIDE OF SANITY

Staring at a crack in the window
through eyes of brooding disquietude,
long and ragged, reaching and screaming
with painful, bitter acrimony,
wondering if this tightrope called sanity
will hold on tight for at least another ragged day...
one more splintered hour exploding with
frantic, pulsing, throbbing angst...
a frightening minute of terrifying imbalance heading
towards safety, or impenetrable darkness...
a thin second of stony silence echoing
against a mind numb and devoid of feelings...
teetering precariously on an edge of swirling shadows
with rust-colored tears trickling maniacally down
clammy skin now just a drab, chalky white...
reeling back and forth, this side light
and that side nothing more than a thick,
oppressive, whispering darkness...
reeling ~ precious balance lost ~ no more
time to worry about sanity or…

Reality has snapped ~ now spinning ~ falling ~
reaching out frantically one last time...
gasping loudly ~ praying to land
upon just this side of
sanity...

THE HOUR JUST BEFORE HOPELESSNESS

Drowning within the seediest, deepest depths of depravity
there is not a speck of light, only shining obsidian,
an awakening that causes the mind to wonder if light
could ever exist, splashed upon an azure sky full of pain.

A dank void of blank expression, insipid darkness so pervasive,
where sinners, lost hearts and broken souls crawl and claw
through a morass of loneliness to echo off splintered minds
lost in a mountain wilderness where only nightmarish beasts exist.

Buffeted by an onslaught of searing wind howling through
cement canyons of cities where fractured lives and ominous death
shuffle across blood-stained sidewalks, stalking those who creep along,
fear radiating like fiery heat from fractured nervous systems.

Resolute eyes downcast because to care is to show concern
and to be humanly concerned is to display stupidity.
To be stupid is to court disaster for when no one truly cares
can the light at the end of the tunnel actually be there?

Or….is it oppressive panic as tortured souls realize that hope
is nothing more than a blind woman, one of society's homeless angels,
living in fear on a street corner with soiled hands outstretched,
hoping for pennies that allow continuance of her fragile existence.

No one cares...only death in reality, for society frowns upon the weak,
sneers wickedly at the lost, sharp fangs of wolves bared, preying upon
the helpless, claws sinking deep into hearts that are devoid of prayer,
staring into empty heavens where there exists only darkness.

Shrieking mountains call out, howls reverberating off wailing walls,
falling upon deft ears, those belonging to public officials
who feel that the blood of innocence should be swept away.

To truly care is showing frailty, displaying hope left for the meek.

Distressful cries of the helpless echo agonizingly off empty hearts,
old ladies dressed in black attire, moaning to mourn the lost,
church candles flickering with the hot breath of demons
led by beasts who revel in sheer delight at the pain of humanity.

When will those who are able to truly care, extend a helping hand?
Will black ashes of the lost cast an evil darkness upon the sum?
Church bells peel out, searching for hope yet longing to be saved,
pure white collars stained with the haunted tears of our young.

A ravenous black cat with slanted yellow eyes stalks the dawn,
searching for scraps of skin and bone rotting in the stench of gutters.
Behind these scavengers preys the sinner man, red eyes glaring
like fallen stars floating aimlessly in a pit of superstition.

It is the hour right before your deepest nightmares become reality,
when packs of feral dogs sniff out fear of the dying, searching
for those who are vanquished, imprisoned within layers of weakness.
Hidden in ivory towers is society, where hopelessness dares not exist.

Swirling and hovering amid the panicky shadows of our fear,
the sinner man peers lasciviously into store windows gaily glittering
with lights that reflect a holiday spirit, when in a reality they are meant
to suck the life blood from the compulsive weakness of humanity.

With a black, beady-eyed crow perched upon his pointed shoulders
the sinner man smiles, rotted teeth dripping blood from devoured souls.
He is the angel of darkness, thriving to prey upon scattered dreams
that barely still exist within the hour just before hopelessness.

MURDER REVISITED

Murderous minds
Underneath moonless skies,
Rage blinding behind soulless eyes
Damnation cries, evilly etched in blood.
Either mine or yours, but does it really matter?
Reckless thoughts of hate and anger now splattered
Right across my heart, split apart by crimson tears.
Either yours or mine, should it really matter?
Darkness reigns where love once ruled.
Remember whispered lonely sighs
Under empty, starless skies.
Murder thus revisited.

The mirror screams...

REDRUM
R E D R U M
R E D R U M

A BULLET HAS NO FRIENDS

Spastic rush hour traffic scurries to escape from Dodge,
lights blinking on and off in agitated consternation,
blaring horns honking like a frazzled gaggle of aimless geese.
Winged rats whose only purpose is to strut, eat and shit upon society.
It's five o'clock amid the dingy ashes of another stressful day
as people lost within this tortured city flee in a state of panic,
wearing their angst on nervous faces like hateful badges,
sweat and tears like blood drained by bosses
with hard, uptight asses.

It's an army of strangers leading bored, monotonous lives.
Winter sunlight washed away, replaced with manic darkness,
depression and fear a thin fragment between nightmares and sanity.
Within the City of Brotherly Love death soon stalks the night.
vicious packs of feral beasts, jacked-up lone wolves,
their bloody paws clutching guns, nervous claws
wrapped around hair-line triggers.
Far off in the distance the plaintive and haunting wail of a siren,
followed by another, then the shrilling scream of one too close by.

It's the sick chorus of any major city, a gothic operetta of the night.
Philadelphia's finest on the move once again in the city where
murder never rests and shooters have no conscious reality.
These cement canyons still echo from a violent shotgun blast,
shattering the jaw of a man in blue, radios blaring "officer down".
A speeding car pulled over, nothing more than a traffic violation.
Yet nothing is ever simple or innocent, the muzzle of a gun shoved
from an open window, flaring and spitting out a spray of birdshot
which does not discriminate, the aim to merely spread destruction.

It's a city in chaos, a mindless mayor speaking from the wrong orifice
where the words, **"Stop, police,"** result in deadly blasts of gunfire.
Down a darkened alley, a scream bounces off soiled walls,
eyes averted, no witnesses, at least no one proud enough to care.
A modern Tombstone, good versus evil, as the innocent stand alone.
This city of cracked and crumbling cement far from glittering Eldorado
as darkened streets and dingy avenues are surely not lined with gold.
Instead, the blood of victims wantonly splashed across cold concrete,
splattered upon walls like a living 'Scream' from Edward Munch.

Down the street where donuts are made for dunkin', a worthless thief
brandishes a weapon, a crazed lone wolf possessing insane eyes,
glaring wide from either crack, an adrenaline rush, or both.
A cop responds for it's his job, an oath taken, forever duty bound.
An explosion rocks the fragile silence as a destructive bullet
seeks the flesh, striking violently, blood and brain matter
splattered across the donuts, sugar-glazed and jelly-filled.
Another officer down, six in two months,
sadly this one killed.

Whether beneath sunlight, or the moon's hungry midnight glow
no one is safe—age, sex, race or creed-doesn't matter, not to evil.
The devil grins, his disciples running wild upon a sordid playground
Reports of gunfire, like kettle drums from an insane symphony
echo down alleyways throughout the City of Neighborhoods,
Philadelphia—Brotherly Love my ass -
more like a malignant Murder U.S.A.
Another tear—filled day, children have lost a father, a wife now
forever distraught will be without the man she loves.

No one near Boot Hill is truly safe as deadly guns are sold on seedy
street corners with hot dogs and sauerkraut, soft pretzels and mustard.
However, the old mayor with the blind eye will soon be gone,
replaced by a new sheriff in town, untarnished yet by the
ruthless slime that continues to overrun city streets in waves.
Even though hope always springs eternal,

it remains a city in chaos, where blood flows wild,
criminals and drug addicts let the muzzles of guns
attached to death-stained claws grin wickedly to spread tragedy.

It's thankfully the sweet demise of another violent day
in glorious Philadelphia, PA, where our heroes in faded blue
continue to wage a valiant battle to place a strangle hold
around the slithering blight of crime,
attempting to halt the deadly spray of bullets
which now and will forever have no friends.
Only death and brutality greedily clutch bloody hands
within the depths of the City, entrenched deeply
in the gutters and smothered in slime.

THE DOOR OF BLACK ROSES

Spidery webs swayed eerily in soft gossamer breezes,
uneasy breath from lost souls pleading, stark light from a silent,
outside world bathing angry, dusty hallways of a frightening
Black Rose Mansion ~ so cold ~ austere ~ icy ~
a malevolent voice loudly wheezing, reaching down
deep inside my soul ~ ~ squeezing ~

Calling out for you! Screaming aloud for me!
I've heeded the pleas to now quietly stand before this
quivering wall in front of the ominous Door of Black Roses.
My hands at rest upon the surface I hear a moan ~ a groan ~
a sultry sigh~ the demon relieved that someone has arrived.
It was simply a long before written destiny!

I stood in awe amid tears of gray, this door of wood
from 5th century A.D., haunting spells hungrily reaching out, alive
with a spirit that pervades my dreams, madly stirring horrid nightmares,
wildly howling aloud my name upon midnight's silvery glare.
A large, hungry black rose in bas relief, surrounded by twelve
smaller flowers, one throbbing and brightly glowing just for me.

Nervous fingers shaking, I touched my rose.
A click that then crashed through my frightened mind.
The door squeaked as it opened wide, my thoughts so terrified,
my God what would I find?
The darkness extended an ugly hand to me ~ a paw of fur~
stiletto claws ~ a growl now whispering my destiny!

Inside the room, I felt the fetid breath of a wolf hotly caress
my neck, hair on my skin hissing, growing, crackling like teeth
of hungry termites, or was it my bones altering shape, body bent
into positions unnatural. I tried to scream, but it was a growl,
my face contorted ~ my mind and humanity no longer
part of man or woman, but that of a beast.

A feral creature howled and roared, slashed and tore
out at anything that dared move in shadows containing nothing
more than primal fears, a nightmarish look at future insanity.
I reached out for the Door of Black Roses to see fading light
swirl down a dusty hallway, distant screams echoing
inside other rooms, or slithering within my mind.

It caressed my skin ~ my hands ~ my face,
all those human traits from that of woman born.
The living Door of Black Roses pulsed and hummed
with a vibrant life not felt before I had entered.
Rising, the small rose I had touched now bled,
the blood revealing humanity all but lost.

Now this dire door called out for those yet to come,
twelve more roses to reveal thirteen frightening destinies
for my nightmare would not be shared alone!

DARKNESS CRIES

Darkness cries good-bye,
your beast howls to blood-red sky,
mourning brings sorrow.

* * * * * * *

Tragic thoughts scream out,
feral eyes in painful shout,
darkness sobs hello.

~ ~ ~ ~ ~ ~ ~

Humanity cries.
Ravens sing in champagne skies.
Tears fall tomorrow.

! ! !
! !
!

Listen as the
darkness
cries

!

SHADOW DANCING

Can you feel it?

Slithering around your ankles like thin bands
of stale cigar smoke, swirling in a grotesque embrace,
dancing a dirty tango against quivering thighs.
Indecent shadows playing a childish game of tag
with fading thoughts of yesterday, mocking fractured dreams
of lost, unrecognized Tomorrow's.

Do you see it?

Through a haunting, whispering darkness, two chilling eyes
stare in a lascivious glare, angry sordid color that of dried blood
splashed across a barren, lonely sidewalk.
The vacant, midnight glow of an estranged street lamp
casting a final, eerie spotlight splayed overtop
misbegotten hopes.

Could it be my blood? Perhaps it's yours.

The sharp glint of something silver floating on the edge
of a pulsing blue light from a searching
police car, shadows dancing gaily
to a song of forbidden destiny.
Long, jagged fingernails claw at the flimsy fabric
of sanity, eliciting a startled scream of terror.

Did you just scream? Perhaps it was me.

The night is nothing more than broken promises
And shattered dreams. A lonely time when fears become the only
life line, sodden with hungry tears grasping for those last threads
of happiness. A howl of forgiveness breaks the silent stillness
as eyes fly open, startled to awakening, darkness floating on slithering
Shadows, dancing on the window to a flickering light of blue.

SHADOWS OF EXISTENCE

~shadows~
crawling furtively
along the floorboards of time,

~slinking~
inside darkened corners
where they weave like insane mimes,

~whispering~
in secret languages
where tongues are split and slither,

~brushing~
against shallow footsteps
placed in this existence now aquiver,

~prying~
trying to claw their way through
an emptiness devoid of dreams and prayers,

~sneering~
leering with a lascivious grin,
scratching inside a frail framework of nightmares,

~echoing~
amid sheer starkness of reality,
pressing against the walls of least resistance,

~silence~
forever dancing, a partner to duality
with these mystic shadows of my existence,

~ or~

may they be yours perhaps

DARKNESS CALLS

The nefarious breath of death
lingers ~ ~ fingers draped across my shoulders
like a clinging, monstrous shroud,
a horrid, malingering cloud
of tarnished dreams.

Sighing, someone's crying out as absolute darkness
whispers in my ears,
grating ~ ~ scraping, scratching down my spine.
Eerie shifting sands of endless time oozing
from a fractured, shattered hourglass.

It's so damn cold in here!
Anguished thoughts shivering painfully within this plea
of supplication, swirling river of salvation
raging~~waging a battle of lost hearts,
reaching out to touch a spark in this feral darkness.

A pin prick of light from within constant midnight,
appearing ~ ~ nearing where I float amidst such anxiety.
Screams of long forgotten dreams assail my senses as I see
a deranged face emerge from darkness, grinning.
It reaches out and tries to touch me ...

I cringe as sharpened talons scrape against my cheek.
These startled eyes fly open, this frantic heart beating insanely
~ seeking ~ peering ~ at my own reflection disappearing
in total blackness, urgent hand falling
frantically across the sheets to lie upon bittersweet rejection.

THE DARKENING

Inside darkened thoughts I pace these halls,
grimmest mask of dire death upon me.
Hear the hiss of evil crying out in tortured minds,
with crimson blade of steel our downfall.

It appears but once upon the bluish moon,
this devilish breath of blackened ash.
Rank stench of blood pervades the air,
my steps the tragic echo of silent doom.

Future hopes are lost ~ this darkened soul as well ~
no point of prayer ~ **Hell** ~ no one left to listen.
I can hear a chorus of inner demons moan a song of death,
haunted howls of midnight wherein only darkness dwells.

House of rooms each painted black, all but save the candled light,
seems to fit this evil heart that breathes within me now.
Blood droplets drip from honed tip of steel
as each bed upstairs reveal such ghastly sights.

Sane thoughts now lost ~ a hiss from **Satan's** sleep.
A tap of tiny fingers now rap upon my door.
Red blade clutched tight, this darkening enshrouds me,
as childish voices echo ~ **"Trick or Treat ~ Trick or Treat".**

THE CROW MAN COMMETH

Darkness reigns
upon these fractured dreams
~~like chocolate~~
bitter sweet upon the tongue.
It slowly sweeps
before these eyes and seems
to block beatific visions sung
in melodies now stained
with blood beneath dark and lonely skies.
Let this silent death
be not the answer wished as
sorrow steals away a final breath.

~~Listen~~

to the blackness creep
upon these broken hearts
as raven wings of darkness
call us home where nightmares
never end in sorrow shared alone.
Sky expands and cries aloud to empty
tears now shed upon tomorrow.
For day is done and night
shall never cease to be,
black wings of death
have swept the
light away.

The Crow Man commeth
soon for me.

Call Me Wolf

A rabid, howling moon reaches out to grab
my strangled throat with craving, hungry claws,
the insanity of lunar midnight now driving me insane.
My fingers curl into nervous, anxious paws,
the curse of being once bitten by infected teeth
bathed in angry, yellow-hooded wolfs-bane.

Searing pain shrieks violently through skin and bone
while beseeching moonbeams scratch and rip away
all straggling shreds of lost humanity.
The sharp echo of altering joints and the scream
of stretching sinew blend together as
call of the wild howls a sad farewell to society.

Nostrils widely flared in anticipating delight,
a hunter's golden eyes now searching for wary prey,
ears twitching forward at the mewling cry
of frightened beasts now cowering in the night.
The dizzying rush of desire for the taste of hot blood
torn from flesh once alive now races through my veins.

The ravenous moon has called my name once more
as I stand in regal silhouette on grizzled hillock,
bathed within the glow of silver moonbeams.
I toss my head skyward, gleaming fangs
snapping angrily at grinning stars
lost in heavens' angry roar.

A growl of primal terror builds to soulful lament as
man and wolf combine to sing in lonely harmony.
The mind of man now locked inside
the shadow of a beast, to rip and claw and tear,
but to forever cry and pray for
everlasting peace.

HAUNTED MEMORIES

Through crimson mist and icy fog
I share my tears to stand alone.
Tis' raven wing and eye of dog
that rips my flesh down to the bone.
I clutch your hand within my fingers,
sweet woman's touch now formed of claws.
The pain of love now lost.....yet sadly lingers....
your name thus whispered from savage jaws.
This human skin now gladly shed
is cast aside like haunted memories.
Your throat exposed as once you bled
through frightful screams and tortured pleas.
I still love you now as I did then,
yet shudder while my beast roams free.
Forever lost upon this bloody path when...
fractured moon cries out to me
in dreams and fog of mystic beast.
Please share my haunted memories
if you so dare...
to share with me the stroll
up angry path of crimson tears.
Behind this mocking door
sobs the memory I most abhor,
the mark of beast upon
my breast to shatter my humanity.
To shower at my feet the fears
that life has ceased to beat
with the beauty thus once held.

So come and take my hand,
or paw... or claw,
and let this wolf of mystic dreams
guide you up to stop and stand
before the altar where we'll share
the blood of beast and man.
Push wide the door that leads to me
and all my haunted memories.

BENEATH THE RAVEN'S MOON

Foreboding wings of darkness spread
as raven soared on thermals of dire dread.
Ominous shadows snaked eerily before the moon
while rays of silver splashed across a scene of deathly doom.

Upon the ground below lay a small, secluded meadow,
stark in horror, ghastly silent beneath a crisp blanket of snow.
One massive and vicious wolf, a baneful marauder,
stood with golden eyes ablaze amid malicious slaughter.

Moonlight glared down upon this frightful scene of death,
fangs of the beast dripping blood through wild and feral breath.
Vengeance now wrought upon the bodies of his enemies,
he howled his rage skyward, a song of pain and lost humanity.

With a startling whoosh of wings came a shriek of sorrow.
Black raven alit upon a barren tree amid the wolf's lonely arpeggio.
Surrounded by carnage and mayhem, the beast stared down
upon the body of his mate, echoes of his tears striking the ground.

Lowering himself, he snuggled against her lush fur, a beast in form,
distraught from the loss of his love, this female once a woman born.
Rising, he altered his shape amid growls of human anguish
torn from snapping jaws, howls of lupine rage spread a top the vanquished.

A raven cawed as shadows crept to the far side of midnight.
Upon two human legs, his bloodied skin glistened in the moonlight.
His life now shreds of torn humanity, now forever lost without his mate.
The man held this she-wolf within his arms, his eyes ablaze with hate.

Falling tears melted the snow around his feet as he said good-bye.
Upon the cusp of midnight, he howled in pain for the woman who had died
Forsaking all humanity, the wolf left in rage, a dark harbinger of doom
as he stalked his prey, embittered and alone, beneath the raven's moon.

KISS OF THE MOON BEAST

For me...while I lay silently
draped quivering within velvet darkness,
the ending was simply but the beginning.
To feel death steal my breath away
on a moon-splashed, neon night
was both frightening and exhilarating.

Clearly I knew what awaited me
as I gazed hungrily into those eyes
of golden, smoldering passion for I was now
enraptured ~ ~ ~ captivated ~ ~ ~ enslaved ~ ~ ~
I remembered the fateful night so well
that it will forever be etched within my mind,
branded for all eternity upon my heart.

Your feral lips brushing mine and whispering,

**"If I asked you for your life,
would you present it to me now?"**

"You have but just to ask," I whispered back.
I felt your tongue snake eerily against my neck
and shivered icily into the vast unknown.

**"If I held your neck within my urgent mouth,
would you scream in unholy terror?"**

"To scream is but to fear, to moan
is simply my deepest surrender," I groaned.
Tensing, I felt the sharpness of your fangs
scratch the soft surface of my skin.

"If I beseeched you to accept the beast,
the wolf who rules the night, would you do so now?"

With frantic heart pounding, I stared wantonly into
a savage face of wild, terrifying, supremely powerful beauty.
"I am nothing but yours to mold and shape,
for with sweet death arrives the pain of rebirth.
Let your hungry kiss be the mark of beast
I so yearn to now embrace."

Fearful, yet anxious, I shut my eyes
to welcome blessed pain to caress me.
Exhaling my final breath of lost humanity,
darkness spread forever until I felt the pounding
of a savage heart and listened to the haunting lament
of a wolfish howl brush the skin of a glorious, silvered moon.
I opened my newly feral, golden eyes and sniffed the air.

"If I asked for your eternal love,
would you merge your beast with mine?"

Glaring into a ferocious night, I howled with sweet desire,
"You have molded me within your own image.
Oh my sweet paramour, this love for you will last into forever"
The moon smiled down with frightening delight.
upon the back of furry beasts now prowling the night.

SHADOW OF A BEAST

As my fingertips angrily strike the keys I see
the longer hands of a shadow moving eerily
in a slightly different direction from my intention.
Extending my right hand, frightening fingertips
of shadow slither like a serpent over the keyboard,
caressing the dark brown, wooden surface of the desk.

Startled, I note that they are elongated and sharp,
like claws of a creature ~ the fanged and furry beast
I write about ~ the beast that forever haunts my
fractured dreams which create my stories.
Glancing through red, sleep-depraved eyes
I read about the innocence that once more dies.

Closing my lids to the burn of tortured insomnia
I pray that I will stay asleep, no more words of death.
**"Open your eyes and write about me, about us,
about the power we possess together, the strength
of unity between humanity and beast. OPEN NOW!"**
The voice was low, guttural, seeming to come from me.

The keys clicked and clattered, driven by fingertips
turned magically into vicious talons, blood on the
'd', and the 'e', and the 'a' ~ can't take this insanity.
My anguished head moves as does the ominous shadow.
Who's shadow? Not mine ~ **CAN'T BE** ~ muzzle long
and narrow ~ it turns, grins ~ drool dribbling on pages.

Heart pounding, I look toward the blurry screen,
harsh, white light glaring, black letters breathing,
like they have a life of their own, fetid breath of madness
so intense it cripples me with fear, fear of what it means.
Darkness squirms to replace the sinister shadow,
last waking moment seeing auburn fur curling upon my hands.

~ ~ ~ ~ ~ ~ ~ ~ ~

The aroma of strong, black, French-roasted coffee
increases my need for caffeine, the elixir I hope keeps
me from sleep and the wild, feral running of beasts.
Reaching for the newspaper I spread the front page.
Startled, horrified, amazed, the headline screams to me.

"YOUNG COUPLE SLAIN IN FAIRMOUNT PARK"
"Witnesses swear they saw a large, wolf-like creature."

Tripping and stumbling towards the desk ~ my haven ~
coffee swilling from the large mug I barely held onto,
I wait with bitter disquietude, fearful of what I'll see.
The stark manuscript appeared and with breaking heart
I read of murder, death and mayhem in Fairmount Park.
Tearfully I saw one long hair still clinging to my hand.

THE RIPPER: KING OF DARKNESS

*** Collaboration with Michael Hawks**

* The great experiment had come to a conclusion.
My journey into this madness of the mind
took me to the great chasm which separates
salvation from damnation, this reason from insanity
and revealed such tender sweet horror.
During just 70 days in 1888, slaughtering the innocent
on the streets of Whitechapel, I became a God.
Worshipped and feared, exploited and hunted.
Never seen! Never found! Never known!
That is, until I received an invitation…

My hand of power clenched as I reached for the door,
ornate knocker in dark, sinister shape of a black rose.
The Mansion stood supremely stoic, gray and morose,
as whispers now called me to stand up for my crimes.
I sneered, for crimes a God cannot commit, feeling
the sensual sharpness of cold, gray steel against my chest,
dried flecks of blood from women spurned it yet caressed.
I banged against the door and open wide it spread,
revealing a malingering darkness that welcomed me within,
evil presence awaiting a God who simply had no sin.

* Stepping into the main foyer of the Mansion
my nostrils flare at the stale pungent odor
of one hundred and fifty years decay.
Long black cloak billows in the breeze
as the heavy wooden door slams shut.
I see the white fog of my breath,
hear my heart pounding against my ribcage.
Flexing my grip on the fillet knife
I move into the heart of this Mansion.

A stranger...yet somehow, I felt at home.
Home within the lustful arms of Black Rose,
her petals like satin, embracing me, erotically sensual.
Little dusty devils whirl like dervishes at my feet
as I slide like the malingering shadow of death,
for I am the final answer to all desires,
the truth, supreme judge and executioner.
Holding the cold, steel blade to my lips, I kiss
the blissful memories of feeling it slice like silk
through sweet Polly's slim neck, her sordid days
of prostitution over, her death sighing within my mind.

* I feel a hand brush against my cheek
sending shivers down my spine,
releasing an erotic sensation not felt in years.
In the darkness, a voice whispers my name.
It beckons me to follow further into
this labyrinth of corridors and staircases.
The black candles flicker as I approach,
then fall silent, as if by magic, when I pass.
The mysterious voice brings me to an oak door,
red glowing letters read, "King of Darkness"

A malignant voice seeps underneath the door,
extinguishing the candles with a hot, fetid breath,
plunging the hall into catacomb-like blackness.
Only KING OF DARKNESS glows a vibrant red.
"Touch ~ the ~ name," the voice sighs wickedly.
I reach and let a nervous hand caress KING.
A click, a whoosh, the door squeaks open
as a white, soupy mist encircles my feet.
A crackling fire casts an evil glow upon a table.
Five women sit, eyes oozing malice and hate.

* A God knows no fear...but I cannot move.
Black hollow sockets where eyes once lived

focus their wretched existence on me.
Their screams ring inside my head
like the thunderous tolling of bells.
I feel my knees beginning to buckle.
I stand defiant to their cause.
I slaughtered these five in Whitechapel.
I will now rip them to pieces in this mansion.
A God knows no fear...for I am the Ripper!

Sliding through the darkened room, firelight glittered
off battered faces, throats slit garishly from ear to ear,
broken mouths frozen in anguished death smiles.
I bent at the waist and bowed, always the gentleman.
"Dear Ladies, so good to see you once again," I said.
~ Mary Ann 'Polly' Nichols ~ 'Dark Annie' Chapman~
~ Elizabeth 'Long Liz' Stride ~ Catherine Eddows ~
and Mary Jane Kelly ~ MY victims ~ MY conquests.
Staring from sightless eyes they pointed to a chair,
head of the table, apt place for the King of Darkness.

* A sterling silver tea set sits on the table.
I notice a spider crawling out of a teacup.
Looking around I begin to notice things.
Cobwebs cover everything on the walls,
the ancient artifacts, paintings, and candleholders.
A fire is blazing, but the room is cold as the grave.
The women point their decaying fingers at me.
I roll my eyes at this obviously cliché gesture.
Suddenly, I am aware that they are not pointing at me,
rather to something which has approached from behind.

I felt the shadow caress my back before it slithered
across my shoulder and onto the barren table.
The air in the room had become abhorrently stagnant,
so dense that breathing became painfully unbearable.
A voice that sounded like distant, rolling thunder

on a stifling summer day cracked the deathly stillness.
"Welcome King of Darkness to this, my Mansion
of the Black Rose," as an icy hand with fingers
more like the white, boney claws of a skeleton seemed
to reach inside my chest and grasp my pounding heart.

* "Time for a God to know fear", it said through rotting teeth
His hand squeezes my heart like a vice
The room spins in a dazzling array of colors
My vision blurs as I feel myself blacking out
In the eternity between the tick and the tock
I experience the zenith of my victims' pain
My body sliced open and the organs torn out
Wide-awake I feel every cut of the knife
My nerves sear in agony as I scream for death
Through this unrelenting torture, the voice speaks...

"So you think your deeds of deadly perversion
entitle you to be called King of Darkness?"
the craggy voice wheezed in a malevolent whisper.
"You are but a sickly gray in the world of darkness.
These unique women sitting at the table before you
did not deserve to have their bodies desecrated
simply because of their sexual indiscretions."
I listened now in abject fear as the hulking black form
standing in shadows behind me beckoned the five grinning
ladies to come forward in order to harvest their revenge.

* Four of these dead decaying women each
take my arms and legs, and carry me out.
The fifth, Mary Jane Kelly leads them
out of the Mansion through a backdoor.
I am helpless as I float under a moonless sky.
Mary Jane opens the gates to a fog-laden cemetery.
I feel prickling tendrils biting at my flesh.
I hear haunted screams of the dead echo from the

tombstones hidden beneath the fog layer.
They let go, I fall but I do not hit the ground.

I'm falling, spinning, reeling down a God-forsaken hole,
screams of drowning souls ringing in my ears,
the evil grins of malicious beasts and demons leering
at my face that is now frozen into a death mask.
My brain is now fractured in fear, skin turning cherry red,
all the hair on my body afire amid the stench of Hell.
Suddenly I stop falling and find myself in the grasp
of muscular arms, skin as rough as sand paper,
the breath of a thousand rotting maggots envelop me.
I gaze up into the eyes of Hell, horns of goat gleaming.

* "What have we here, a little god?"
he says as he sets me down
on the banks of the River Styx.
I watch bodies of the damned float by,
their screams for mercy are ignored.
The Demon leans in close and whispers,
"Jack, I've been waiting for you."
I have had just about enough of this.
Reaching into my coat pocket
I grasp the handle of my fillet knife.

The silver blade became alive within my grasp,
humming and beating with a life of its' own.
Scotland Yard cried that I had killed a mere five women.
So blatantly wrong ~ for I AM the KING OF DARKNESS.
Many more had been slain and perished underneath
this hooded and steely gaze, slaughtered bodies
of no importance littered the gutters and storm drains
along the dark and foggy alleyways of London's
Whitechapel. Now for my biggest conquest
as I plunged the knife into the Abyss behind me.

* I slice the demon's neck clean through,
then hook my right arm under his
and hurl him over into the River Styx.
I hear his howling laughter behind me
as I run through the labyrinth of Hell.
I come to a bridge that crosses another river.
Beyond this bridge, I see the Black Rose Mansion.
At the arched doorway, Baron Von Crow smiles.
I stand here perplexed at the sequence of events
that has transpired on this most irritating day.

Looking behind me, I can see the glow
still oozing though the ground in which I fell,
screams of searing pain and haunting doom
echoing from the angry bowels of hell.
Walking towards the Black Rose Mansion
the rooms are alive with light and warmth,
something this home has not had for centuries.
I stopped before the doorway, my mind confused.
Why had I received the invitation to come here?
The Baron smiled, "Welcome home my son."

*The Baron reaches out and puts a hand on my shoulder.
I sense his thoughts as he touches my mind.
In the infinite time between heartbeats
everything from the moment I became the Ripper
to standing at the entrance of the Mansion in Hell
is made clear, and it is only now I realize
that the Mansion is a living breathing entity.
It chooses who will enter through its doors.
Those dark ones chosen, the truly dark few
must prove their worth, or face the wrath of the Mansion.

I stared with hard gaze through darkly hooded eyes
at this ancient, yet frail man who seemed to be my father.
It was now crystal clear to me that the monstrous shadows
hovering over me during my fractured childhood
was this man who called himself Baron Von Crow.
I had always wondered where light ended and evil
darkness began, how killing became so insignificant.
Do I love him, or hate him? No matter, for he would be dead
soon and the King of Darkness would rule Black Rose Mansion.
It would live through my blood and all would bow to me.

THE END

THE GATEKEEPER

~ ~ Darkness looms ~ ~

on broken brow, my tragic soul
hath long departed, no longer me
with body drained of all life sustaining
organs. Thin shaft of light, so deadly bright,
reveals a Door ~ the Gate ajar ~ a Portal to
dark Underworld, black eyes of death
now sordid bound, devoid of love
upon whispered tears amid
heartless scorn, this sad
and broken life afloat
on water red, ahead
the tombs of ~ ~

~ ANUBIS ~

Lord of the Dead,
the Keeper of the Gate,
the path to Cynopolis *City
of the Dogs* his breasts the form
of woman born, as the head of Jackal
grins and leers with hooded eyes of pity.
I gazed through shades of fear, seeing bodies
spread on icy slabs of stone, sharp blade of blood
within his hands, now soul released to float away
upon a dark River of the Dead, once human
shell now filled up by the Embalmer,
sweet Guardian of the Veil.
continued on next page…

~ ANUBIS ~

the God of Dying,
our Patron of Lost Souls and
Orphans, awesome Lord of the Dead.
As I float away to who knows where, I see
my heart placed with loving care upon the scale
to be measured with the feather, praying that my heart
is light and presented to Osiris, for if the heart be
heavy, then the horrid mouth of Ammit doth
open wide, crocodile teeth with the hiss
of cat thus devours the soul I once
possessed amid the screams in
the Hall of Two Truths.

Upon the Throne
in darkened veil sits Thoth,
frightening Prosecutor of the Dead,
while Osiris looks on upon the final court,
this judge that will determine if my deeds within
this life were good enough to be lighter than the feather
of Ma'at, Goddess of Truth. I try and hold my breath
of which I have no more, worried that my heart
be too heavy as my soul will be soon devoured.
Osiris stands stoic with arms spread wide,
for the feather has not moved. My
soul thus saved and now held
within the dark hands of

~ ANUBIS ~

NIGHT OF THE SPHINX

Bewitching time is but the sweet breath of night,
feral whispers sifting from a silvering moon
awaiting the explosion of a vibrant sunrise.
She calls forth to defile the beguiled,
sweet demonic daughter of the Chimera ~ ~
intoxicating Mistress of your fate.

Moving to the swirl of biting sands
with the sway of haunting palm fronds,
she dances ~ she twirls ~ she spins to evil madness ~
the pounding heart of a lion surging to come alive,
bathed in moonlight before pre-dawn's awakening,
nighttime breezes singing loudly for beasts to thrive.

Listen closely to the crackling winds ~ ~
can you hear the lion's ravenous roar?
The moan and groan of hunger to be appeased,
carnal need to feel just one more sacrifice desired
by the lioness beast who is part woman born,
with the wings of a bird and serpent's lashing tail.

She slides with silent grace through dark of night
seeing another victim walking the trail of shadows.
The she-beast whispers into his unsuspecting ear,
"Which creature in the morning goes on four feet,
at noon on two, and in the evening upon three?"
The riddle left unanswered, his heart belonged to her.

Soft fingers that caress like silken threads,
hands of a strangler flexed with brutish strength,
she revels in the power of one more conquest met.
Her magical beauty used to mesmerize and enchant,
demonic appetite thus sated with but one more
devoured soul, fresh taste of blood upon sweet lips.

In her twitching cars a fading beat from a dying heart,
consumed by human frailties, deceit and lies.
Roaring at a golden, resplendent moon she unfurled
her wings, soaring into darkened sky towards the morn
of another approaching blood-red and tangerine sunrise,
her urgent desires satisfied, her hunger now subdued.

Gliding upon angry thermals, long wings spread wide,
sinister shadows brushed a shivering earth below.
Night after night her lion roared as death begets
more death, souls once lost upon the living now
within her chants the song of everlasting life,
for she is the Queen of Darkness, Demon of Destruction.

Came that fateful night she asked the question,
"Which creature in the morning goes on four feet,
at noon on two, and in the evening upon three?"
Oedipus smiled for he knew the answer to destroy her.
"Man—who crawls on all fours as a baby, then walks
on two feet as an adult, and with a cane in his old age."

With a painful growl that rumbled across the ground,
an angry roar that thundered though the heavens,
and a shriek that stilled all human heartbeats,
the she-beast cast her body from a ragged cliff,
the demon now devoured by lost souls within her ~ ~
terrifying night of the Sphinx to be no more.

Yet still ~ ~
when silvered moon hangs high the dark breath of night
caresses me, a growl rumbles from deep within my breasts.
Wild lion craves to stalk the streets as raptor shrieks
to flee the nest. The demon beast will rule once more
for an innocent soul this night will surely die a horrid death.

UNDER MOONLIGHT'S SPELL

(Collaboration with Brian Damon)

Heels clicking upon the lonely pavement,
stars at night humming a moonlight sonata,
strangled thoughts adrift upon tortured dreams,
my life so distant from what it once had seemed.
New found power surging through trembling hands,
nervous fingertips now a' tingle in electrical sensation.
Steel bars surround a dark, sinister cemetery whispering,
"Oh, Sweet Maritha, would thou commeth to me?
Take thine hand so we both may become alive."
Soft hands upon the gate as it opens wide ~ ~

With a wicked eye cast upon the gate,
the vampire stalks...forever cursed to walk
within the confines of this bleak cemetery.
He gazed hungrily upon this new possibility of prey
as she stepped into view through the creaking entranceway.
Something foreign assaulted his senses.
It was the newborn power flowing within her blood,
the very blood that may set him free.
Shivering with anticipation and bloodlust
the vampire began to plot his next move ~ ~

I could almost touch the insipid presence
that seeped deeply into my tingling skin.
And yet ~ ~I felt so drawn towards this magnetic voice,
a voice of pure strength and supreme domination,
of frightening possibilities and unequaled sensuality.

The moon-kissed tombstones seemed to breathe in response
as my necromantic powers whispered to the graves.
I was the last remaining witch of my coven,
all others sought out and destroyed ~ ~ I was alone!
Joshua waited, sharp fangs echoing their urgent bloodlust.

Watching as Maritha slowly walked among the graves,
resisting the temptation to take her by force
and ruin his chance at freedom for another century,
Joshua continued talking to her mentally ~ ~
promising, threatening, begging and demanding,
anything to get her willingly into his grasp.
The intoxicating scent of her power-laced blood
was almost more than he could stand
as she unknowingly passed within a few paces
of Joshua and his lust for her newly found power....

Dazed and confused, I stopped and glanced about,
hearing the dangerous whispers wriggling within my mind.
It was intensely erotic, yet ever so silky, eerily powerful,
drawing me further inside this dark, ominous world
of dingy headstones, broken crosses, and haunting crypts.
The many dead literally begged me to release them
so they could but walk the earth under moonlight once more.
Magical blood boiled in these veins like molten quicksilver.
My mind was a' swirl with thoughts of lust and desire,
but for What reason, and for whom? Spinning about I stared ....

Centuries ago a young woman, much like the one
now standing before Joshua, cursed him to walk forever
within the ancient grounds of the cemetery.
Caught in the act of draining the life blood of her sister
and damning her soul to eternal Hell on Earth,
she spoke in tongues from the Grimoire.
The power of her words shook the foundation
of Joshua's soulless body.

"The kiss of your kind freely accepted not once,
not twice, but thrice on a moonlit night shall set you free."

Staring into the mist I detected a most imperceptible movement.
Then he magically appeared, seeming to float above the ground.
He was stunning, beautiful, mesmerizing, and so very powerful.
I was drawn to those blazing red, feline eyes ~ a predator's eyes,
like an inquisitive mouse eagerly hungering for a hunk of cheese.
My powers seemed tame compared to his, and yet ~ ~
he grimaced as if in pain, lifting an arm to repel my advance.
The voice of my great aunt whispered a dire warning,
"Beware my child for this is the beast that slew my sister,
your great grandmother. Dare not let him drink of your blood..."

Realization of the alluring scent flowing from her body
was one that he had tasted before.
It spread a grimace of pain across his face.
Joshua still felt the searing agony coursing through his veins
with blinding hot light as the first sister spoke those terrible words
that sealed his fate~ to walk destitute and alone within this cemetery.
Feeding of small vermin and insects, barely enough to sustain existence.
had made Joshua only a fraction of the predator he once was.
Knowing it was now or never, his mind filled with subterfuge,
he raised an arm in mock submission,
preparing for battle that may never come.

My power cascaded around me in wavy, pearly-blue light.
At first it was blinding, hot to the touch, throbbing with urgency
to make physical contact with this one-time Master ~ now fallen ~ Vampire.
Fear was alien to me, yet I knew this evil beast
had begun the steady destruction
of our coven and the curse upon him sill needed to be consummated.
With his right arm upraised to repel my unique abilities
I glanced to Joshua's left and saw the bloody bodies of two young girls,
their slim necks ripped open as if his hunger had become too voracious.

"The kiss accepted not once, not twice, but thrice..."
Pulling back my hair with neck exposed ~ I smiled ~ his eyes blazed red…

Pure unblemished alabaster skin gleamed in the moonlight
as Maritha pulled back her hair and tilted her head.
The animal instinct of the Vampire's mind screamed for more.
The fresh and powerful blood pumping within her veins
would break the seal on his curse and allow his freedom.
But...would he survive?
At what cost was this freely given chance from one so powerful?
Joshua realized that to be free of the curse was worth caressing her power.
Upon her desire, Hell would be her destination...
fangs sinking into her neck.
This could perhaps be the worst mistake he had made over centuries…

The pain was severely intense, yet softly erotic.
With jade-green eyes shut tight, his kiss was most exotic.
In my mind, a sharp prism of light blazed stunningly bright, while
sweet visions of mother's exquisite face danced before me.
Lonely tears mingled with desire, my heart beating madly
as I realized how Joshua had savagely slaughtered her.
Teeth feasting upon my neck,
I sliced open my own wrist with tapered nails.
Moving in a circle, I spun the beast around
as blood dripped to the ground.
While he sucked and slurped, the circle of power became complete.
Now this creature of the night was mine ~ ~ revenge can be so sweet.

Panic stricken, Joshua realized too late that something was amiss.
Swirling thoughts within his mind could not grasp
the total and absolute control this necromantic witch could
possibly have over him, the power drawn from her ancestors
and their lust for vengeance against the vampires responsible
for reducing their numbers to only one known survivor.
With a sigh, Joshua removed his fangs from her neck and tried to rise
only to find he was unable to move all but his terrified eyes.

Maritha began to softly chant,
calling forth the fallen family of sisters for upon
this night, she felt nothing could stop the moonlight spell,
not even Joshua.

The sky became as black as the deepest obsidian
while streaks of lightning appeared to spear the silver moon.
Thunder rolled across the heavens~ footsteps of angry gods.
Once haloed ground beneath my feet began to quake
as bony fingers of the dead broke through the crusty earth.
Standing over this fallen, despicable creature, I raised my hands
to the night and chanted,
**"Upon this fateful night my Queen of Darkness,
giver of power and beauty, sweet Goddess of Death
and Destruction, your servant, Maritha of Eldergon,
humbly seeks the strength to consummate
the curse placed upon this vile, wretched creature at my feet".**

Within a shimmering blue light arising from the fog covered ground
rose the dead bodies of twelve women, those from the past
who had been destroyed by Joshua and his evil brood.
Forming a circle around Maritha and Joshua
the twelve spoke as one, **"Little sister, our wish has been fulfilled.
The Vampire responsible for the atrocities against our coven
lies powerless at your feet. Let us join our power
to yours and finally destroy this harbinger of destruction."**
An unearthly light spewed from each of the twelve witches into Maritha.
She could feel power and strength
overwhelm her as she pondered Joshua's fate.

With arms raised high, sharp colorful streaks of light
touched my fingertips.
Sheer power from the dead, combined with my own, was staggering
The Sisters of Eldergon chanted in one voice,
rising like rolling thunder

My mother, Corrinda, smiled and nodded,
knowing her death was to be avenged.
The circle of twelve dead sisters began to revolve,
like a ghastly carousel.
slowly at first, then spinning faster and faster, chanting over and over,
"Goddess of the night, avenge our deaths, resurrect our coven."
I felt harsh light and heat envelop me,
my auburn hair appearing to be aflame.
Joshua lay curled up in a ball, glancing up at me through terrified eyes.
It was but a ruse as he used his remaining power to summon his brood.

As the corporeal forms were returning to the
twelve sisters of the Eldergon coven.
Joshua, using his mind-speak called for the warriors of his brood.
From out of the South appeared his warriors numbering seventy or more.
Blood thirsty fiends, brigands, and morally corrupt creatures of the night
hell bent on the final destruction of the powerful Eldergon coven.
Like a pride of hungry lions, the vampires quickly surround the witches.
Silence permeates the magic filled air as Maritha pulls a wooden stake
from the folds of her cloak and presses it to Joshua's chest.
Ripples of fear began to roll in waves off the bodies of everyone,
permeating the air and marking time like the tick-tock from a clock.

I raised my head with eyes blazing red, then blue, then red again.
Left hand grasping the stake, the right hand surged power into my sisters.
Through glowing eyes I could see their skin covering glistening bones.
As Joshua's brood crept ominously forward on silent feet,
I spoke aloud.
**"Sweet Goddess of Darkness,
we call upon thee now through Sword
of Theraclese and Claw of Draminous,
upon the winds and air of northern
stars and blood-covered daggers,
help your humble servants raise the dead
from their silent sleep and bring to bear the
Wolves of Eldergon to destroy**

this evil brood and return Eldergon
to thy glorious veneration and reverence."
The ground rumbled and split apart while howls rent the silent night.

Grizzled and bony fingers forced their way up through the ground
at each and every grave ~ clawing, digging and pulling ~
clearing the ground away so that their bodies could be free.
Under moonlight's spell the animated corpses appeared maniacal,
sightless eyes and vacant sockets glowing red with the fury of rage.
At the disturbance of their supposed permanent slumber,
seeing and sensing other un-dead creatures, but somehow different,
these reanimated specters from the grave attacked with a frenzy.
Watching this vicious assault upon his brood
Joshua summoned what little strength he had left and made his move.

The ancient cemetery was like a god-less war zone,
yet the powerful spell thus
cast kept the manic slaughter and mayhem away
from human sight and sound.
With my eyes blazing red,
I saw the zombies clad in their tattered clothes
grappling with Joshua's hellish brood, their un-earthly moans mingled
with the hissing of pissed-off vampires, heads and limbs being ripped
and tossed through the electrified air like a gang of manic fruit pickers.
The Wolves of Eldergon attacked the vampires
with savage claws and jaws.
Suddenly, I felt Joshua grab my legs and pull me
to the ground, breaking contact
with my twelve Eldergon sisters,
the creature's gleaming fangs lunging for my neck.
I called out to my wolf as the beast leapt
from within me in a thunderous roar.

The magical wolf, summoned by Maritha,
seemed to explode from her chest
with a howl that would chill the reapers soulless bones.
Surprised and shocked, Joshua instinctively pulled away as
the wolf stood between him and Maritha's now unconscious body.
While the battle raged on around them these two monsters of the night
eyed each other, preparing for the attack. Moving as one, both began to fight.
snarling with gnashing of teeth, saliva dripping from fangs.
Neither could top the other, equal in their duality of life and death.
Suddenly, Joshua stopped as the twang from a crossbow rent the air.
With a wooden arrow shaft protruding from his chest Joshua fell to
the ground.

Through waving layers of consciousness I heard my wolf howl.
It was the haunting song of victory as the beast commanded the pack
to stop they're vicious slaughter and return to whence they came.
With a sharp intake of breath and a gasp,
my wolf leaped through my chest
and returned to the safe confines of my body and mind.
I opened my eyes.
The cemetery had the electrified air of burning wires
and coppery smell of blood
As I slowly rose, Joshua moaned and I stared at the
arrow imbedded in his chest.
With a groan and holding onto the shaft,
his dead eyes pleaded for mercy.
"Please Maritha, do not let me die.
We should be together forever."
Another voice spoke, "Maritha?"
I turned to stare at Rhamonda, my Great Aunt.

"The arrow within his chest has been poisoned,
for him, with cold dead blood.
Already he is dying, leave him be.
Command the dead back into their graves
and return to their slumber, never to be disturbed again.
The Sisterhood of Eldergon
has come full circle as prophesied by the Grimoire,
and Warlock Vastonne.
All but you, and I, shall return to the
spirit world until summoned again."
Hearing Rhamonda's words, the twelve sisters of the past slowly faded
leaving Maritha full of their amazing power.
The raised dead returned to their graves
while the Earth swallowed the remains of Joshua's
once mighty brood. With the Vampire
sprawled dying at her feet Maritha turned on her heel,
and with a breaking heart
walked away. Behind her,
two blazing red eyes glowed with hatred and lust.

SHORT STORIES

DON'T EVER PICK UP ROAD KILL

It was eerily dark as I drove cautiously along a very windy, many times treacherous Manor Road. What made it even more foreboding was a **thick**, lathery fog which made it seem like I was driving through a handful of shaving cream. It clung hungrily against the ground, thus making driving just a teensy bit precarious. In fact, the whites of my knuckles wrapped around the steering wheel made that fact clearly evident. A swirling layer of creamy white mist crept just high enough to lap gingerly against the broad hood of my '94 Caddy. Why in the hell did I come this way? I swear, sometimes I'm just a complete idiot. But here I was, like it or not, praying that I didn't suddenly come face to face with the startled black eyes of some large deer with a death wish.

I mean seriously, it was a tad misty down along River Road which ran right beside the Schuylkill River, but the dense fog didn't really start until I began climbing the hill towards the golf course. This eerie road had a history of weird stories, the most notorious being the one where the locally infamous Elmo Smith abducted a young girl in the early 1960's from Ridge Avenue, brought her here for an evening of rape and murder. If my facts were somewhat correct, he was the last person to be executed in Pennsylvania back on April 2, 1962. Up until 1913 the preferred method of execution had been slipping a rope around your neck with the Keystone state being the first to abolish public hangings. However, inside the walls of county jails 'private hangings' were still conducted. But weird, old Elmo who was obviously three bricks short of a full load had the distinct pleasure of sitting in the electric chair with a metal salad bowl upon his head, a black cover over his face, and enough juicy current to grant him the final thrill of a lifetime. He was also the last individual to be executed in Pennsylvania.

Suddenly an icy chill ran up and down my spine as I realized it was near midnight on April 1st. Oh my God, why in the world did I come this way? Even though Barren Road was probably soupy too, it would've been much better than traversing this insane route. Then I remembered reading a horror novel titled "Raven's Way" by some weird Philadelphia writer that had a chapter where a young girl was killed by a werewolf along this very road after striking a deer and crashing into a ravine. Quickly my knuckles got whiter, brown eyes got bigger, and my heart began beating even faster.

I slid the window down on the driver's side so that l could stick my head out in order to get a clearer view of the road. Doubtful I would have to worry about hitting an oncoming car head on because nobody in their right mind could be as stupid as I was. All the high beams did was blind me as the bright light exploded against the swirling fog. The low beams were not much help either. However, what I found to be really kind of weird was that the sky above was actually sort of clear so a full moon did glare down at me. Shaking my head, I figured that was quite appropriate as my gaze searched for the next hairpin turn.

So there I was, driving along a road that was dangerous at best in any inclement weather, creeping along at a meager five miles an hour. Suddenly there was a hard jolt along the right side of the car, like I had struck or run over something large. I slammed on the brakes and came to a jarring halt. Thankfully I had my seat belt on, but that didn't stop me from jamming my right wrist against the steering wheel.

I sat there for a few interminable seconds, afraid to even breathe. The first thing that hit me was how damn quiet it was. Well, all but for that strange pounding sound in my ears. Then I let out my breath and realized it was my own heart thudding against my chest. Sitting back, I unlatched my seat belt, but kept the car running and the lights on. In fact, the hell with it, I put the high beams on as well. More light the better I figured. Opening the door, I nervously let my left foot sink into the fog, anxiously reaching for purchase on the damp pavement. Once there I pushed my reluctant body out of the seat and stood somewhat erect on shaky legs, my back against the car.

Okay, think girl, think!! Calm yourself down damn it. Maybe it was just a log or a large rock. Yeah, that's all it was, especially since there were lots of trees along this road and I remembered having to steer around many branches torn from trees after a severe storm. But... I had to know for sure because that's just the way I am, sometimes overly inquisitive to a fault. Keeping my right hand touching the fender I started to shuffle towards the front of my powder blue, 1994 Cadillac Deville and then slid along the hood where my hand suddenly struck the emblem. That brought me somewhat out of my fright-induced state. Breathe damn it, breathe!! I took a few more tentative steps until I came to the other fender. I very slowly extended my neck, cocking my head and looked down towards the ground. The fog swirled around, making it difficult to see anything clearly. Then there was a slight opening in the soup and I saw something large and brown underneath the car. Oh crap, I realized I had run over a deer that had evidently been lying on the road. Great, this was just fantastic. Sometimes if I didn't have bad luck, I wouldn't have any at all. Now I had to either back up over it and steer around the carcass, or drive forward letting the back tire bounce over the body. Either way, it was going to be horrible, but I realized I couldn't stay here. Lord only knows what kind of creepy things could be out there staring at me, ready to rip and tear my body apart. Damn, now I was really scared.

So I began carefully guiding myself back along the fenders and hood towards the wide open, welcoming front door of the car. Suddenly a loud screech from an owl I suppose broke the silence and I screamed. Jesus, I didn't think I could scream that loud and oh my how it echoed throughout the naked trees. My heart thudded louder and a tear broke free to trickle down my cheek. Oh man, I had to get the hell out of here. I scrambled quickly to the front door of the car and jumped in, slammed it shut and clutched the steering wheel very tightly. The blood in my knuckles completely disappeared and they were bone white again.

Shoving the car into first gear, I touched the gas pedal, much harder than I really wanted to. The car burst forward as the rear tire pounded over the dead deer. It was road kill anyway so I figured somebody else could pick it up if they wished to. Daddy had always told me never stop to pick up road kill, even if I was the unfortunate one to hit something. But I had heard stories about goofballs picking up dead animals for their hides, antlers, and yes, even a good meal now and then. Yuck, no way, not for this girl!

My body violently shook back and forth in the seat from the jolt as I realized I had forgotten to put my seat belt on. I kept going however because nothing was going to stop me now. The hell with it, that deer was deader than a door nail and I needed to get home where l could pour myself a very large glass of wine, maybe even two or three. For all I knew I'd be hearing wolf howls any minute and that would just about give me a freaking heart attack. I realized quickly that I needed to slow down or I'd go careening off the road like that girl in the novel.

That was clearly not a viable option. It was good I did because not more than twenty yards or so down the road, right in the middle of my lane, stood a young man with really red hair. I yelled loudly and slammed my foot on the brake pedal, way too hard I might add. Without the seat belt clutching my shoulders my chin struck the steering wheel hard enough to bring tears of pain to my eyes. I fell back into the seat and then threw the door open.

Jumping out of the car with the headlights illuminating the strange young man standing in the road, I yelled at the top of my lungs, "What the hell are you doing? Do you feel like getting killed or something? Are you crazy or what?"

Obviously I'm sure I sounded quite insane myself so I waited for a response. None came, not even a smile or an angry glare. He just stared back at me with this haunted, vacant look. Maybe he was hurt I suddenly thought.

"Hey, are you okay? Sorry I yelled, but you scared the crap out of me. I already ran over a dead deer right down there so I sure as hell didn't need to smash into you," I scolded him in a much lower, more normal voice than was reasonably expected.

Continuing to not get a sensible response other than a blank, nobody's home, stare, I leaned forward and insisted, "Hey, hello, I'm talking to you."

He turned his eyes to stare at me and that was when I saw that his shirt was torn and muddy, along with his trousers and shoes. I didn't see any blood, but that didn't mean he wasn't hurt. I moved away from the car and walked towards him. However, when I got to about three feet away from where he stood I did see some scratches and blood on his face and arms.

"Oh my God, you're hurt, what happened?" I asked quietly, afraid to startle him. "Did you wreck someplace? Can you talk at all?"

He tried to crack a thin smile, but it didn't work since it was more like some evil grin. But at least it was a physical response nonetheless. "Yeah...I'm okay...I think. At least...I'm walking anyway so I guess.

I'm alive...right?"

"Well, unless you're some kind of crazed zombie, I would think so," I shot back. "So what the hell happened? Where is your car?" I inquired, glancing around more than a little apprehensively.

He motioned robot-like with a thumb over his left shoulder. "Back there someplace...off the road. I think I hit...a deer maybe...darn, I hit something."

I started to laugh, the nervous sound bouncing around through the thick mass of woods. "Yeah well, I also hit the damn thing, but it was thankfully dead already. Do you need a ride; can I take you someplace? Call the police, a tow truck, or maybe your family? You look like you're hurt."

"A ride...would be great. I live close by...just off Ridge. My father can come back...with me to look at the car," he replied in a somewhat droning, very unemotional tone. "If you don't mind...that is. My name is... Keith by the way. Just Keith I guess."

"Well, mine is just Sheila and no, I don't mind at all. In fact, I'd really welcome the company driving along this road tonight. But seriously, you honestly look like hell. Are you sure you're not hurt too bad? It's no problem at all to run you down to the hospital."

He shook his head slowly, like it was very stiff, and then moved his hand in slow motion up to touch his forehead. "No... I'm okay I think. Just some numbness...no pain really. Can we leave now?"

"Sure, do you need help getting into the car," I asked him.

"No... I'll be fine," as he shuffled forward, kind of sliding his feet along the damp pavement, just kind of staring into nothingness almost.

I slipped back into the car beside him and slammed the door closed. Made us both nearly jump out of our clothes actually. Putting the car into drive I slowly started forward, wondering what next might lunge out at me. I could only pray it wasn't that horrible werewolf from that really scary novel I had read.

I noticed as I drove very cautiously through the fog that he sat very stiff and eerily quiet. Suddenly feeling extremely nervous, I saw him turn his head to glance out the window. Raising my hand to cover my mouth and with a loud gasp I could see that nearly half the back of his head was missing. I could clearly see a blob of gray matter, obviously exposed brain.

That was when he turned to face me. The strange grin I had seen earlier when he was standing in the road was more than just evil and his eyes belonged to somebody who was very much dead. Oh shit, I realized right then and there that I was in deep trouble.

As my screams echoed through the dense fog, the very dead zombie with flaming red hair reached out hungrily for me. I knew in a split second I was going to die and all I could remember in that instant was my father telling me on more than one occasion, "Honey, whatever you do when driving, especially at night, don't ever pick up road kill."

THE END

THROUGH THE EYES OF A BOY KING

February 3, 2007 was bitterly cold and blustery. A harsh, biting wind swirled around the corner of 20th Street and the Benjamin Franklin Parkway in center city Philadelphia, brisk with an overbearing feeling of ominous trepidation. Eric Tuttler stood with hands stuffed deeply inside the pockets of his dark gray dress coat, not only to keep them warm, but to conceal the fact they were shaking so badly. In fact, even handsomely clad in his best suit with a blue tie that was strangling him at the moment, he still shivered and not merely from the frigid temperatures.

Standing frozen at the bottom of cold, pristinely white, concrete steps in front of an imposing Franklin Institute Science Museum, he gazed up at six tall stone pillars. Inside was what he had dreamed of seeing for so long. Now it had become more of a nightmare, though he was very careful not to reveal his fears to anybody, especially his parents. After all, who would believe that this world renowned boy king, the youngest but the most well-known of all the pharaohs, had been whispering to Eric in his sleep for many months now?

It was the opening night gala for the Tutankhamun Exhibit, Golden Age of the Pharaohs. Philadelphia was the final city on the U.S. tour and promoted as the last and best location to view this marvelous exhibition before leaving for most likely another ten years. The Franklin Institute had been founded on February 5, 1824 by Samuel Vaughan Merrick and William H. Keating in memorial to the great statesman and inventor Benjamin Franklin. The esteemed and notable architect, John Haviland, was hired to design the original building located at 15 South 7th Street (now home for the Atwater Kent Museum of Philadelphia). But the most recognizable part of The Franklin Institute open to the public is The Franklin Institute Science Museum. After vacating its 7th Street building, the Institute opened at its current location on the Ben Franklin Parkway in 1934.

Women strolled and strutted on the sidewalk, clicking like chattering castanets on high-heeled shoes, both outside on Market Street and inside the historic museum, looking elegant and graceful in their long, colorful dresses, glittering jewelry, and a vast array of furs to keep them warm. Men paraded in handsomely constructed suits and tuxedos, some looking as uncomfortable as a wind-blown colony of penguins.

Six months ago you'd have thought that Eric would've been absolutely giddy, literally floating on a cloud of excitement, his infatuation with King Tut being as strong as it had been for such a long time. On his bedroom walls at home hung numerous pictures of the boy king. while his desk held statues and the shelves contained books on the history of this most famous Egyptian pharaoh. His buddies at school had been calling him Little Tut or King Tuttle for several years, especially after he had presented a stunning paper and in-depth exhibit on King Tutankhamun during his sophomore year of high school for history class.

As a deepening throng of animated people moved about on the sidewalk and the steps, Eric was nearly oblivious to the jostling and excited chatter around him. His heart was pounding wildly and his palms were actually wet from nervous perspiration even as chilly as it was outside. The corner of his mouth curled subtlety into half a smile. He realized that today was his 18th birthday so you would think he might be happy, which he was to a certain degree. But upon awakening so abruptly from another disturbing dream he had been having almost every single night for weeks, the thought of it being such a milestone in his life was rather meaningless.

Long time patrons of the Franklin Institute, his parents had quickly marked this date upon their calendar when it was announced that the King Tut exhibit would be coming to Philadelphia. The fact it would be opening on their son's 18th birthday was almost too good to be true. Both his parents were extremely proud of Eric, his mother always telling him from a very young age that he was destined for something very special. She would often point to the small turquoise, crescent shaped birth mark in the middle of his right palm and say, "Honey, this mark here means something very special, that you were destined for greatness."

However at the moment, greatness was the furthest thing from his thoughts for he was frightened in a way he had never been before. Eric could do nothing more than clutch his right hand into a tight fist. Since Wednesday his hand had been burning with increasing intensity. All throughout today it was actually throbbing, as if it possessed a life of its' own with a vile, evil heartbeat.

Suddenly, a heavy gust of wind struck him so hard he nearly lost his balance. Those milling about the sidewalk, including his family, gasped in shock and alarm. As it died down, a distinct whisper assailed Eric's ears. Come to me, I've been waiting so long for you!

Eric quickly looked around in surprise, startled at the clarity of this strange and ominous voice. He had only heard it before while deeply lost in sleep. but never when he was awake during the day. His nervous expression was evident to anybody who might've been glancing his way.

Seeing the frantic look upon her son's face, his mother asked, "Honey, are you okay? That gust of wind shook everybody up for a few seconds."

"Yeah mom, I'm fine. Did you just say something a moment ago?" he nervously inquired, "before you asked how I was?"

"No, just when I asked if you were okay," she replied, trying to rearrange her long blonde hair.

"Now, it's time to go inside. Are you excited sweetheart?"

Eric hesitated, not sure of actually what to say. He had become so obsessed with King Tut that this moment should be the apex of his long-time interest in the boy king. Now he was completely terrified, as if his shoes were deeply encased in wet cement upon the sidewalk, unable to move a muscle.

Not wishing to disappoint her, he replied, "Sure mom, I'm very excited, just really nervous I guess. Thanks for everything."

She smiled and grabbed his right hand, squeezing tightly. Eric winced. hoping nobody saw the grimace of pain spread across his face. The words, "Come to me, I've been waiting for you!" continued to echo through his mind.

Hugging her son, she smiled, "Happy birthday Eric. I love you so much."

He mumbled back, "I love you too mother," as she began moving gracefully up the steps to the massive front doors leading to an event he seriously wished to avoid.

Once inside the high-ceilinged foyer Eric was stunned. The room was awash in color and contained a high buzz of excitement. After presenting their tickets, Eric moved through the crowd with his parents and four-year-old sister, Jessica, towards the coat room. Still shivering, he didn't really want to relinquish his coat. He just silently prayed that these feelings of dread would pass and he could enjoy the night with his family. After all, it was his 18th birthday, a special time when heading towards adulthood.

As they made their way through the crowd, Eric held firmly to his mother's hand and Jessica clutched tightly to her father's strong fingers, her mouth agape in complete awe. The room was filled with dignitaries, the who's who in Philadelphia society. Eric spied Governor Rendell smiling and shaking hands, always the politician, but forever a Philadelphian. Across the vast room Eric caught a glimpse of Matt O'Donnell and Tamala Edwards from channel 6abc. While outside his father pointed out the evening anchor Jim Gardner standing with reporter Erin O'Hearn. So the evening was replete with the rich and famous rubbing elbows with all the other attendees lucky enough to capture tickets for this gala event. Then there was Eric he thought, smiling to himself, just your short, rather cute, but kind of geeky looking, extremely gullible young man. Destined for greatness his mother always told him. Somehow he doubted that, more like heading towards some degree of weirdness.

He certainly wasn't hungry, especially since his stomach felt like the inside of a turbulent whirlpool, but his father had managed to get the attention of a waiter precariously holding a tray of hors d'oeuvres so Eric took a few crackers with some kind of paste on them just to be polite. Realizing it was some kind of pate' he wanted to spit it out, but knew he could not do that so he swallowed with disgust. He immediately washed it down with a full glass of soda.

Each of them had grabbed a program upon entering so they would know where most of the more than 130 artifacts from Tut's family (including 50 objects from his tomb) were elegantly on display. Eric thumbed through the brochure, his interest being more and more piqued. Awesome relics from over 3,300 years ago, much of it so well preserved that it appeared the items were made recently. Of course, the mummified body of Tutankhamun still rested within a small tomb in the Valley of the Kings. As far as anybody knew, King Tut was the only pharaoh still entombed there.

In order to try and stay somewhat calm Eric let his gaze scour the milling crowd while his parents talked to several lawyers who practiced with his father. Surprisingly, his eyes settled on the long, luxuriant red hair belonging to Katie Springer who was in several of his classes. Eric had always thought she was absolutely stunning and he desired so much to ask her out on a date, but his constant state of shyness around girls kept him from that massive undertaking.

His friend Christopher told him she had mentioned some interest in Eric and that he should talk to her. Chris thought it would be a blast to double date. However, he was more relaxed listening to the powerful whisper of King Tut haunting his nights than dealing with girls who he thought were much more dangerous.

Suddenly, Eric's sight started to get blurry as a quick burst of light exploded behind his eyes. Spreading before him was a vast desert, rolling dunes set in the distance, a burning sun bouncing off glittering sand as it swirled around the agitated feet of milling horses and camels. Standing proud upon a white chariot sparkling with gold filigree, attired exquisitely in a white hunting tunic with red trim, stood King Tutankhamun holding a long, curved bow. Encircling his neck and chest was a collar of shining red and blue pieces inlaid upon a gold base. Upon his head sat the famous Nemes head-dress, spread about his handsome face like an expanding snake with the protective cobra and vulture upon his brow. Though he stood a mere five feet, six inches tall and was slight of build (coincidentally the same height as Eric) this commanding king radiated power and authority.

As quickly as the light exploded behind his eyes, it disappeared. Eric reeled, shaking his head and stared ahead, squinting at the brightly lit room he had been standing in before the vision. His father grabbed Eric's arm with a concerned look on his face.

"Son, what's wrong? It looked like you were starting to fall forward."

"It's nothing dad. I haven't felt all that good today and I guess the closeness of this crowd got to me a little bit," Eric said, smiling as much as he could.

"Then let's get out of this mob and start walking through the exhibit. After all, it's what we came for, right?" his father smiled back, putting his long arm around Eric's shoulders.

"Yep, I'm ready. There are lots of items I'm dying to see," Eric replied, almost wincing painfully at the word 'dying'.

So they began weaving their way through the crowd, being carried along like floating upon a river of despair, at least for Eric. His stomach was lurching and he could not figure out why. The mark on his hand was burning so badly now that he had his fist clenched, pain radiating up his forearm.

As they moved from room to room and down hallways, the items on display captured his attention, enwrapping him in the awe that was King Tutankhamun's legacy. The glitter of gold seemed to be sparkling everywhere. Eric could hear voices all around him, marveling at the items, but the words were mostly unintelligible. As he stood before each magnificent piece it was as if he was looking through another pair of eyes. Nearly from the beginning, a swirling haze encircled his gaze. rippling on the edges like those concentric circles in a pond radiating out from the toss of a rock. He was startled at first, then became more nervously accustomed to it. He also didn't understand quite why. but he was beginning to feel this powerful aura about himself. Certainly nothing this geeky, fairly handsome, somewhat shy boy had ever experienced before.

Eric stared at each item, oblivious to his surroundings. There were the funerary beds made of gessoed wood, each one gilded in gold. One was constructed in the shape of a cow, totally covered in gold with black spots and an impressive pair of horns. Another was comprised of elements from a hippopotamus, a crocodile and a leopard. The one he now stood silently in front of was mesmerizing, each side in the shape of a lion, beautifully constructed with the head of a lioness on each side. Ironically, the inscription on the mattress read Mehturt who was a cow goddess. However, on the frame of the bed was inscribed the name of Isis-Meht, a lioness goddess. It was thought the engraver possibly transposed the names in error.

A dark voice whispered in his ear, "This was meant for my rebirth whose time is now."

Eric passed silently a stained ivory headrest, elaborately decorated chests, boxes and cabinets, each so equally impressive. One item that caught Eric's eye was the Ankh Shaped Mirror Box. A little further on he stopped and stood, the rippling around his gaze shimmering eerily. Before Eric was the golden throne of King Tut, the heads of lions protruding from the arm rests, and on the bottom of each leg were the impressive feet of a feline. The chair was carved from wood, covered with gold and some silver overlay. It was intricately inlaid with colored glass, semi-precious stones, faience and calcite. Upon the back of the chair was the picture of a king and queen.

"This is where I sat and ruled a magnificent empire. Young Eric, this power will soon be yours."

Eric moved as if in a trance, unable to conceptualize his thoughts, the haunting whisper a constant drone in the back of his mind, seeing Tutankhamun's wealth with an appreciative gaze not completely his own. He found himself standing before an item that made his eyes widen while blood rushed through his veins like a turbulent river. It was the golden death mask of the boy king.

The mask glittered in solid gold, beaten and burnished to a powerful luster. This mask had been placed over the head and shoulders of the mummy, overtop the linen wraps that totally encased his body. The eyes were narrow with an almost effeminate shape of his nose, a slight smile of fleshy lips, and a strongly chiseled chin. It was the countenance of youth, an approximation of Tut's portrait.

The stripes on the headdress (nemes) were of blue glass, also used for the inlay of the plaited false beard. Upon the brow of the mask was a vulture's head. Made of solid gold, the beak was comprised of horn-colored glass, but the eyes were missing. Beside the vulture was a cobra, also composed of solid gold, the head made of dark blue faience, inlaid eyes of gold cloisonne with translucent quartz overtop a red pigment. The hood of the snake was inlaid with a combination of carnelian. lapis lazuli, glass-colored turquoise, and quartz. The black, beady, ferocious eyes were made of quartz and obsidian. The vulture represented sovereignty over Upper Egypt, and the cobra ruled over Lower Egypt. Upon the chest of the mask was a broad collar extending from shoulder to shoulder, encrusted with lapis lazuli, quartz and green feldspar with a border of lotus-bud and colored glass.

Eric stood silently, both stunned and awed at this marvelous nemes which was the proposed facial construction of King Tut. In his mind he asked, "Is this really you?"

A hiss, a whisper, "Yesssssss, it is I, soon to be we."

Erie felt the crescent mark on his hand begin to burn more intensely causing him to glance down. The mark was now a beet red which caused his heart to pound even harder than it had been for the last several hours. It wasn't really painful to the point he couldn't stand it, just extremely hot, almost sensual.

He suddenly felt light pressure upon his arm and glanced up to see his mother smiling and voicing words he couldn't really hear. All he could do was smile back and nod, being led toward a destiny that he both dreaded and yet mysteriously looked forward to.

For the next half hour they casually strolled and stopped, admiring so many of the exhibits. Questions were being asked of Eric constantly, some he heard and answered, others he just ignored, mostly due to the increased buzzing within his head. They passed a game called senet, placed in the funeral vault so that the deceased person would have something to occupy themselves with. Eric explained to his parents that the game had a long history, depicted often ín the scenes on walls of Old Kingdom tombs, nearly a thousand years prior to the death of Tutankhamun. Eric felt himself smiling and yet sensed it was not he who was grinning.

They strolled past toy boats carved from wood with great precision, one with rigging. There was a gold dagger and sheath, King Tut's royal scepter, a bronze trumpet, an ivory headrest among other types, an ostrich feather fan, a model boomerang, a votive shield, rattles used in rituals, and a wonderfully magnificent gold gilded wood chariot.

In another room were the boy king's crook and flail. These items were separately discovered when the tomb was opened, the crook found in the antechamber and the flail within the treasury. The flail is historically the more interesting because it bore on the gold cap at the base of its handle the king's name in its early form of Tutankhamun. It also stated Nebkeperura, the king's throne name.

Eric explained that to some experts, this showed the flail had belonged to Tut while he was still a child, yet after he took the throne. Possibly it had been used in his coronation ceremony at Amarna at the age of nine or so, but before he was crowned at Karnak. The crook, commonly used by every shepherd in their daily lives, held significant symbolism to rulers of that time. The crook's name in Egyptian is 'hegat' with 'hega' being the common word for ruler.

There was stunning jewelry in glass cases such as necklaces, bracelets, anklets, earrings, buckles, pendants, rings, amulets, pectorals of vultures and scarabs, all exquisitely made of gold and precious stones. As he stopped at each piece Eric touched his wrist and chest, as if he could actually feel wearing these stunning items.

As they turned a corner and entered another room, pain exploded in Eric's head. He reeled backwards and threw his hand out to touch a wall, praying not to fall and bring attention to his plight. He quickly regained his composure, but like what had happened in the main foyer, Eric was not seeing what was actually around him. Instead, he found himself aboard Tut's chariot, hurtling over a grassy plain pursuing several lions, a huge male and a beautiful lioness. Beside the chariot, running easily with grace and power, were two large, brown pharaoh dogs, heavily studded collars encircling their necks.

The king's driver yelled and whipped at the horse, driving him harder and faster. Tut held his bow, arrow nocked and ready to fly straight and true, prepared to bring the boy king yet another honorable trophy. As they turned quickly to avoid a small copse of trees, the right wheel came loose, spinning and bouncing up against a large rock where it splintered apart. The right side of the chariot crashed to the ground, being drug by a terrified horse as a thick cloud of dust spread over the savannah. King Tut was recklessly thrown from the vehicle, flying through the air to land heavily, rolling over and over until he came to a back breaking thump against one of the trees. As Tutankhamun gritted his teeth in pain just before he passed out, his gaze caught a black chariot coming to a stop. Standing ramrod straight, grasping tightly to the reins of a nervous and prancing horse, was his military commander and master charioteer Horemheb. The boy king reached out for help, his fingers quivering in agony. Waves of dizziness overtook the king, his head bleeding down his back from a deep gash.

As he reached out to grab his left knee, only to find it sticking out through the skin, he yelped in pain and looked deeply into the eyes of Horemheb which glittered with treachery, an evil smile spread across his face.

Eric's legs began to crumble as the room came back into focus. A yell from his mother caused his father to reach out. Quickly though Eric stood straight and felt fine. He looked around and smiled sheepishly, embarrassed that he had become faint and had caused a slight commotion.

His mother took hold of Eric's arm and said, "Come on, we're going home. Something is wrong Eric and you need to lie down. Tomorrow morning I'm calling the doctor."

"Mom, I'm fine, really. Please, I want to finish going through the exhibit. We're almost done anyway," he replied, patting her hand. "I can rest when we get home and if I don't feel okay in the morning you can call the doctor. I must've just got the bug that's been going around the school. Please?"

"Oh Eric, I don't know. If you feel you're okay now then we'll finish, but I'm keeping my eyes on you," she tried to say sternly, followed by a loving smile. "When we get home you're going straight to bed."

"Yes mom," he replied, whining just a little, gripping her arm and tugging her forward. Her motherly protection sometimes was overwhelming to him.

But underneath this false sense of bravado his stomach was churning and his fractured mind was reeling. That was the second time this evening where he felt he was actually in Egypt, watching King Tutankhamun in a scene that seemed he was literally acting out through Tut's eyes. He knew that he was far from okay physically as he had told his mother, but something was magnetically drawing him forward. It seemed to seep into his skin like something wicked, an evil and powerful force that had him captured in some mysterious spell.

As his mother had firmly stated, she had one eye on the exhibit and the other set squarely upon her son watching for any sign he might become faint again. Eric smiled, always aware that he was able to manipulate her with just a twinkle in his eye.

He loved both his parents, but he had always had an extremely close and affectionate bond with his mother. Perhaps it was because he was always the shortest kid in the neighborhood, constantly avoiding bullies when he was much younger, not sports oriented at all, and quite frankly, a true nerd and bookworm. So much of his time, at least until his senior year in high school, had been spent at home reading and playing the piano. During that time, he and his mother had many heartwarming talks, especially since he never felt comfortable talking openly to his father.

Moving through a doorway into a darkened room Eric stopped cold and gazed alarmingly, but with complete awe, at a display that was simply breathtaking. He felt like he had seen and touched it all before.

Within subdued light, as if it was still within the canopic shrine, stood the canopic chest. The beauty was marvelous in a pristine way, giving admirers a treat they had never hoped to see. The chest was carved from one solid block of semi-translucent calcite, delicately hand-crafted on a background of dark blue pigment. Upon the lid was a winged solar disc of Horus-of-Behdet. The four corners of the splendid chest were decorated with images of Isis, Nephthys, Selkis, and Neith.

Within the chest were four stoppers in the shape of human heads. They stood quietly in pairs, the two on the east faced west and the two on the west looked towards the east. The heads were fitted tightly above four cylindrical hollow spaces. These were Tut's canopic jars, each holding a linen-wrapped, resin-smeared coffinette made of beaten gold. It was these jars that were to hold for eternity King Tutankhamun's internal organs. The liver was Imsety, the lungs were contained in Hapy, Tut's stomach contained in Duamutef, and Qebhsenuef held the intestines. These were named for the four sons of Horus.

The room was exceedingly quiet as if the patrons of the exhibit were moving slowly in a state of total reverence. Eric stood before the jars, totally and completely mesmerized, oblivious to the people who stood around him. Within his head came Tut's voice, no longer a whisper, but a strong and powerful sound.

"You have come to me at last. Your destiny was pre-ordained many years before your birth. Now my young Eric, gaze hard at Imsety and concentrate for you are to witness my death as well as know who the evil traitors were. Then, and only then, can you and I become one body, one mind, one spirit, one powerful fist for revenge and domination."

Eric went blank, again seemingly taken from his body and transported back to over three thousand years ago. The large room was dark, lit only by numerous flickering candles. It was deathly quiet. The only sounds to break the ominous stillness were the king's labored breathing and moans of pain. One doctor administered to Tutankhamun, basically going through the motions of attempting to keep his ruler as comfortable as possible.

His hands had been basically tied from the beginning when the injured body of their pharaoh had been conveyed back to the palace. His orders were to appear as if he was doing all he could to save Tut's life, all along however permitting the infection from his severely broken leg to become worse and savagely ravage his body. Beyond the fact the doctor knew he would be killed if he fought these orders, he was also promised great wealth and stature.

Off to the right of the large bed stood three figures steeped in shadows, only the flickering light from the candles exposing a traitorous eye, or a nose, or part of an evil grin. The powerful figure to the left was Horemheb, the commander of Tut's army and his chief charioteer. His face showed no mercy, no compassion, or regrets. It was he who had sabotaged the wheel on his pharaoh's chariot. His plan had worked to perfection.

A much slighter figure of a man stood quietly to the left. This was Ay, Tut's high adviser, and the one who primarily ruled Egypt, the power behind Tutankhamun. He had hated and despised Tut's father, the powerful Akhenaten, who believed in worshipping one god, or monotheism. He worshiped Aten, the sun god, and had a new capital built at Amarna. To many of his followers, including Ay, as well as the powerful priest-hood of Amun, this type of devotion was heresy. After Akhenaten's death, Ay returned to Thebes with the boy who was now to become a king, nothing more than a mere child himself. At the high adviser's secret directions, Tut brought back the traditional gods, those much more popular with the priesthood and the Egyptian people.

Horemheb had powerful motives and would eventually become pharaoh, but not until after Tutankhamun's death. Tut's high adviser, Ay, would become the next pharaoh of Egypt. Ay knew he should've been made pharaoh, not this whimpering boy, but the child was Akhenaten's sole héir and next in line to become leader of all Egypt. Being as young as he was, Tut could've ruled for many years, thus keeping Ay from what he felt was his rightful place in history.

Between these two powerful and traitorous men was a smaller, much more demure figure. This was Tut's wife, Ankhesenamun, who had been lured into the plot recently. She resisted at first, fearful that her husband would find out and ensure her death. But she was young like Tut, though more gullible and easily manipulated by someone much stronger and supposedly wiser.

Plus, she was exceedingly lonely since Tut seemed to always be away on hunting trips and visiting far parts of their realm. Ay had made her believe that a future filled with happiness and power was at his side. Now she wasn't so sure, fear and worry gnawing nervously at her stomach. However, what terrible deed they had wrought would soon become reality. She would marry Ay who would become pharaoh upon Tut's demise, his murder thought Ankhesenamun sadly.

The boy king moaned upon his death bed. He knew he was dying and was prepared to be received and warmly welcomed by the gods. In fact, during these days of terrible agony and mindless meanderings, his father Akhenaten had visited him during what had become crazed dreams. It was during these eerie visitations that his murder was revealed and who the traitorous killers were.

The pain and fever had placed him in extreme delirium for most of these last two days. Now, his mind was cloudy, teetering upon ragged layers of consciousness. He remembered the sneering leer on Horemheb's face when his chariot had crashed. There were the whispered orders to the doctor from his 'trusted' advisor, Ay, instructing the physician on things not to do in order to save the pharaohs life. Finally, there had been the cunning deceit in his wife's eyes and the protective way Ay placed his arm around her shoulders.

Through tiny slits he stared at this treacherous trio and with what final strength remained in his ravaged body he lifted his hand slightly to motion them forward. The crescent mark on his right palm blazed angrily.

With reluctance they shuffled the few paces to stand beside his bed, the vile putrefaction from his rotting leg assailing their senses. Horemheb and Ay winced, while Ankhesenamun covered her nose with a lacy white handkerchief.

With his final breath, King Tutankhamun whispered as loudly as possible for all of them to hear his final words.

"As I stand before death's door, I know of your deceit. You have slain your leader, your supposed friend, your loving husband. Upon this revelation, hear me clearly. I curse you all until the day you die," Tut whispered, his words broken and failing. "My body may have failed, but my soul will live on. Know full well until your dying days that I, King Tutankhamun, will avenge my death against your families no matter how many centuries it may take."

Upon these final words the king's last breath was expelled in a long, terrifying hiss. The room became deathly silent and Ankhesenamun began to sob. Horemheb smiled in victory, knowing that his own power and stature would finally become reality. Ay closed his eyes briefly and let the king's curse seethe within his mind, knowing full well the power of hate.

The light in front of Eric's eyes began to shimmer and explode with color. He did not know if he was standing or had fallen, simply that a powerful force had now entered his body. It was the presence of greatness, but the pervasion of evil. A voice, the one he had become so used to hearing over these past months, rang clearly through his mind.

"Awake Eric, for now you know the treachery that sealed my fate. I live again through you. We have become one powerful, overwhelming force. Eternity is ours and vengeance will be wrought, no matter how long it takes. I have waited over three thousand years to live again," echoed the words of King Tutankhamun within Eric's mind, body, and soul. "Open your eyes and see the world for what it now has become. You and I together will rule nations. People will bow before us. Open your eyes and live."

Eric's eyes fluttered opened. Gasps of fear could be heard throughout the crowded rooms and hallways. Upon the possession of Eric's body by the spirit of Tut, the lights had flickered on and off menacingly. The popping of bulbs could be heard throughout the building. Women screamed, children cried, men shouted.

Booming thunder could be heard outside the Institute, rattling windows and shaking the very foundation the building sat upon. Icy rain began pelting the streets in a torrential downpour, terrifying streaks of lighting splitting the sky apart. A volley of sirens throughout the city echoed off frigid city walls and empty streets, a strange symphony conducted by powerful, unseen forces.

In no less than ten seconds the lights within the Franklin Institute flickered back on and the terrified voices began to subside, though the riotous stampede towards the front door continued, just not as frenzied. Outside upon the street, Eric's mother stared at him while his father held a terrified daughter.

"Honey, are you okay? How are you feeling? I was yelling at you inside the building and you were completely unresponsive even though you were talking in a language I could not understand."

Eric turned to her and smiled lovingly. "Yes mother, I feel fine. In fact, for some strange reason, I feel better than I have in quite a while. Let's go home, I'm suddenly very hungry."

As his father steered the car through traffic on the Expressway towards their home in the Roxborough section of Philadelphia, Eric stared through the window at a peaceful Schuylkill River. The storm lasted approximately ten terrifying minutes causing extensive damage throughout the city. Weather forecasters were at a loss to explain this sudden terrifying phenomenon.

However, through the glass Eric gazed at his own reflection. He realized something miraculous had happened. The power within him now raced with wild abandon through his veins and somehow he knew it was because of King Tutankhamun. That he, Eric Tuttler, was no longer just a shy, insecure teenager. There was a presence of royalty and nobility within him now. To his alarmed dismay, there was also a malevolence eating away at his mind, a vengeance and evil foreboding that he was still unprepared to accept.

A soft voice whispered within his unsettled thoughts. "Don't worry Eric. Open up and allow the power of pharaohs to lead you into the future. You have become the most invincible force in the world. Together we will rule and avenge my death."

Eric's mouth broke into a sly grin as he thought of what his mother had so often told him throughout his young life of eighteen years. That he was destined for greatness. How prophetic her words had now become. Settling back in the seat he gently closed his eyes. He was suddenly extremely tired, yet exhilarated, for the world now awaited.

THE END

1313 DARKLING WAY

A dirty, grayish-black mist with swirling wisps of sickly yellow, the stagnant color of putrid bile, hugged the earth tightly with claw-like tendrils. An insipid, deranged evil whispered through the bushes. This malignant menace echoed frighteningly against naked trees now stripped of their dried-up, leafy attire. Nearing the cusp of midnight, wintry temperatures had dropped to below freezing with the fresh scent of snow riding the crisp air. However, the ominous presence of a power rarely felt before made the air so frigidly cold that fragile human skin would simply crack and split open, blood slowly dripping to the ground where it would immediately freeze upon contact to turn jet black, the other color of repugnant bile.

Suddenly a deep, animalistic voice crept across the disquieting stillness. Starting with a low growl it began to rise until windows along the lonely street rattled from the force of a terrifying roar. This evil presence was extremely old, other-worldly ancient, and as the sound subsided there began a hideous choking, a violent retching and clearing of phlegm that would normally signify death. Yet this hideous, incorporeal entity was already dead...if it had ever been alive at all. For sure, it moved fiendishly among humans with exterior form and substance, but the beast was simply clad with skin and bone stripped from his multitude of victims. It was an outer crust from those unfortunate humans who mostly had to die savagely in order that he could continue his nightmarish existence and continued depredation.

Now it stood stooped over, haunting midnight shadows caressing a body that was wrinkled and withered like sea-worn leather tarnished from salty air. The ultimate need for fresh blood had sallowed his skin, turning it a sickly yellow mottled with splotches of a dusky, gray-blue. Around the creature's shoulders clung a shroud of the four humours of ancient and medieval medicine.... yellow and black bile, phlegm and blood. Though the creature had once been an esteemed physician who had stood shoulder to shoulder with the great Hippocrates, Plato, and

Aristotle, his never-ending need for blood also made him the utmost purveyor of death.

The Hippocratic Oath was nothing more than empty words, becoming twisted and insane, attune to his own torturous existence. Life and death were one in the same to the beast for to respect life was to honor death. To experience being alive was reveling in the thrill of dying, feeling the sweet flow of blood from another's life force satiating a nightmarish need, often becoming purely orgasmic.

Wheezing painfully, coughing up a tar-like substance that reeked of inner-decay, the monstrous apparition realized it needed fresh, sweet blood and quickly. It glanced slowly to the right beyond the metal gate which led to an imposing structure that was beyond the preconceived image of a haunted mansion. Upon each side of the ornate, steel gate were the stark numbers 1313. The undead creature felt exhilarated to once more be surrounded by crisp, nighttime air and yet it hungered for the gentle warmth of his crackling hearth. A hearth to be sure filled with stark-white bones, blackened pieces of skin littered amid the ashes of far too many innocent victims.

The beast returned a hungry gaze toward the empty street. His dry, cracked lips slowly peeled back into a hideous grin exposing brilliant white fangs, probably the only part of his body that could not decay. From the corner of his ghastly mouth crawled the wiggling head of a large maggot which he voraciously bit in half, swallowing the morsel with gusto. Good God he was hungry, though God would surely not condone the feast he was about to greedily partake.

From a house along the far end of the street a first floor light blinked on, followed shortly by the opening of a squeaky back door and the soft woof of a dog. The creature felt a thrill of excitement as the scent of prey caressed his quivering nostrils. Letting the large black cape covering his shoulders fall to the ground, the beast allowed his wings to unravel and then stretch out, thin leathery membrane between the digits and phalanges flapping slightly in the breeze, much like a sheet hanging outside to dry on a clothesline. A low, keening moan escaped his wretched mouth, the sound of desire and urgent need. Sharp claws upon his feet dug easily into the frozen earth as the creature pushed off effortlessly into the air, the thrill of the hunt upon him once again.

The winged beast coasted silently upon a strong breeze, slowly circling with anticipation the unsuspecting victim with murderous intent. This monstrosity that preyed upon human life was a darkling, a murderous spawn of Satan, and was the oldest of demons. It had been created out of malice and hatred, to wreak havoc and devastation upon Lucifer's enemies. The Prince of Darkness had called forth an army of demons to be led by the darklings. Soaring lower and preparing to strike, this one was named B'haliel. It was the most ancient and one of only six darklings powerful enough to remain permanently away from the roaring fires of Hell.

With a mighty flap of wings, the creature dropped with dizzying speed. The man heard a whoosh of air and looked up. There was only a second of horrifying realization before the beast's talons struck, imbedding themselves into the man's head and neck causing instant paralysis. This allowed the victim to stay alive, unable to move or speak while the body was later slowly drained of blood, then devoured. Using another clawed hand, the creature struck the golden retriever which had time to issue only a weak whimper. There would be no evidence left behind. blood or severed body parts, which had always been the way of darklings. Nosy police could always poke around, but never with sufficient evidence to accuse. If they got too pokey, then they disappeared as well.

The beast's powerful wings easily carried its' prey over the imposing steel gate toward the mansion at the end of the street, 1313 Darkling Way. B'haliel's stomach growled with anticipation for not only did he need to feed, but this shell of a human body had to be revitalized, serving him well over the last two hundred years. Eventually it would have to be discarded in order to find another vehicle, male or female, didn't really much matter. When outside the human crust, the beast was nothing more than a dark shadow, able to slink and slither undetected until it struck with surprising ferocity.

But for now, it needed to gorge and quickly. A large, double window on the third floor had been left open for easy ingress while clutching prey in more than one claw. The room was large and mostly empty, containing only one oversized easy chair set in front of a welcoming fireplace. No need for additional trivial items for this was the creature's feeding room, far removed from the formal dining room downstairs where he entertained for special functions. After all, he had to maintain a decent modicum of respectability among his circle of society.

Even though the man lying upon the floor couldn't move, barely able to breathe, he was still alive. Terror filled his unblinking eyes as the creature lowered a savage head, exposing fangs tingling with excitement. Sinking easily into the victim's neck with scalpel-like precision, the beast slurped and gurgled, rolling its' demented eyes into the back of their sockets. When the body was completely drained of life-sustaining blood, the darkling proceeded to dismember and continue to feast, discarding the bones into the roaring fireplace with any leftover pieces of skin that was noisily disgorged.

Within an hour the only evidence remaining was a large blood stain upon the tiled floor which the beast lapped up with gusto using a large, viper-like tongue that was split at the típ. For an after dinner treat, the demon slit open the dog's stomach so it could succulently devour the heart and liver. Fur, skin and bones were discarded into the fire, now roaring with hellish glee.

Moving slowly toward the easy chair the beast relaxed, feeling his skin become rejuvenated and the bones in his body reclaim their strength and vitality. Above the fireplace, tilted slightly down, was a mirror. B'haliel was satisfied to see the handsome countenance of a dashing young man in his middle thirties, enough to make ladies swoon and males jealous, but extremely wary.

He fell asleep as the morning sun swept across the front gate of 1313 Darkling Way, illuminating a sign that read: Dr. Demian Satana, DO, Internal Medicine, Obstetrics & Gynecology. He had several appointments scheduled for the next day.

THE END

IF ONLY FROGS COULD SMILE

A solitary tear meandered lazily down her right cheek where it gently merged with one from the other side. Together they converged as one into a larger bead that balanced precariously on the tip of the young woman's exquisitely sculpted chin. Glancing down at the pond, she stared wistfully at the beautiful face floating upon what seemed like an endless sheet of glass, a mirror without end, an eternity free of sadness. Wondering if she would ever again touch the warmth of such an eternity, she took the tip of her right index finger and wiped at the wetness in the corner of her eye. Then she gently guided a few wayward strands of glistening auburn hair that had fallen in front of her face to lie neatly behind her right ear.

The quivering tear broke free, spinning and twirling toward the pearly surface of the water. She knelt upon the lush park grass and softly spread her butter-cream colored skirt with dainty red roses gracing the hemline. Her stoic, emotionless face of beauty was intent only upon seeing a reflection of the tear hovering in mid-air like a magical crystal sphere, suspended as if in the slowest of motions. But fell it did nonetheless, pointed towards a placid pond of shining water, its' sole purpose to shatter the lovely early spring stillness that surrounded her. It was simply a pleasant moment in time, one that did not come often for her anymore. After all, happiness had been tragically stolen from her on a day much like this sunny afternoon exactly one year before.

The tear violently struck the water, sending shock waves of concentric circles across the small pond, cracking the exquisite beauty of her face. It distorted a vision of loveliness into a caricature of horror. Using the same index finger, she touched the ugly, livid-white scar that knifed glaringly down the right side of her face from just above the brow to underneath the chin. Physical pain had fortunately disappeared six months ago, replaced with nothing more than an icy cold numbness spread across her otherwise smooth and faultless skin. However, the emotional pain of loneliness and loss would apparently linger forever, sharp pangs of despair part of each lonely, agonizing day.

As the rocking water began to stretch out and become placid once again, she tried to smile and then quickly stopped. Stupid girl, she thought, trying to actually have a split second of frivolity, a breath of time when her torment might perhaps flee. Smiling did nothing more than turn the white scar into a fractured lightning bolt, the tortuous pain of seeking forgiveness knifing down her face and neck, pointed towards her anxiously beating heart which was now and forever constantly broken.

Remembering that fateful afternoon was merely one troubled aspect of her daily, zombie-like existence, one she wished that she could forget, but seemingly doomed to live out the curse which had befallen her. As she closed her eyes trying to forget, but realizing the absurdity of that wish, the sound of croaking frogs echoed inside her thundering mind, the roaring sound always appearing when the nightmare began.

It had been early evening like this one, a blush-red sun sinking slowly behind the western horizon. She and Christian, her fiancée, had attended an all-day pool party at her friend Deanna's lavish home. She really had had a good time, at least until the beer and whiskey chasers had begun to take their toll on Christian. Extremely handsome at slightly over six feet, his rugged good looks were the envy of all her friends, especially when he slipped off his shirt and stood upon the diving board, his sculpted arms and stomach glistening under a bright sun. She felt her cheeks become pink as she noticed how the tight fitting swim trunks he wore left absolutely nothing to the female imagination. Hearing startled gasps of desire from many of the other envious young women around the pool was more than just a little satisfying, especially since Christian could've had his choice of girls, but had chosen her.

Handsome, personable, charming, and financially very successful, he had it all and she had him, most of the time wrapped around her pretty little finger. Sadly, the one thing he lacked however was the ability to control his drinking and no matter how hard she had tried to slow him down, it had just gotten worse. Now she sat pushing back in the car seat, holding on tightly to the door handle with one hand and seat belt with the other. Christian swung the steering wheel hard to the left as they careened onto Seventh Avenue, the vehicle hurtling down the semi-busy street past Long Acre Park on their right side. Fortunately, it was Sunday evening so any rush hour traffic was not in harm's way.

"Chris, please slow down. You're driving like a madman, somebody is going to get hurt," she uttered loudly, strain and fear etched clearly in her voice.

He laughed, a high-pitched, keening sound, much like a madman would. "Lighten up baby, have a little fun. I can always control this car."

"Christian, you're drunk. Pull over and I'll drive home, please!"

His head swiveled and he stared at her, a crazed look of anger and mis-trust. "Katie my dear, drunk is in the eye of the beholder and I'm beholden to nobody. Just sit there, look beautiful, and be quiet."

She was stunned for at no time had he ever spoken to her like this, drunk or sober. For some reason he was like somebody she had never known before. The thought struck her that maybe there was more to his condition than just booze.

Suddenly, a movement caught her attention and she looked forward. A scream began to build which erupted from her throat.

"Chris, watch out, there's someone crossing the street. You're going to hit them," she yelled shrilly.

He turned his head back to the pavement and saw a woman with a small boy holding her hand halfway across the intersection. The red light glared back at him like an accusing eye.

Chris shouted something unintelligible and yanked the car to the right. With less than ten feet to spare, Katherine saw the terrified look on the mother's face as she tried to protect her son from what appeared to be certain injury.

The out of control vehicle jarringly struck the curb and lurched onto a large, square cement area erected in front of the pillared entranceway to the park. Since Christian had still not applied the brakes the car sped forward doing nearly fifty miles an hour.

Katherine screamed but the screeching sound of metal striking the stone pillar on her side drowned it out. The entire time, which literally was only seconds, Chris attempted to regain control of his BMW, but it was no use. His drunken condition left reflexes and mental capacity nothing but mush. Their lives were now at the mercy of fate.

When the car had slammed violently against the stone pillar, Katherine's body lurched up and forward even though she was wearing a seat belt. The top of her head struck the metal strip around the windshield causing an immediate burst of stars and a flashing stab of pain. Stunned, she fell back onto the seat, feeling like nothing but a rag doll that was now bleeding profusely from a deep gash across the upper part of her forehead.

The car now hurtled down a wide sidewalk which abruptly turned right with a log fence standing impassively in front of them. They smashed into the fence sending fractured pieces of wood flying in every direction. Ahead was nothing but grass and Long Acre Pond. Christian was now completely dazed and so rubber-armed that steering the BMW was impossible so thinking enough to press down on the brake pedal was out of the question. Fortunately, his foot was not on the gas so the car had at least slowed somewhat.

The entire time, people who had come to the park to spend a nice spring Sunday afternoon were yelling and screaming, scurrying for safety. The car was like it had been shot forward on a pinball machine, glancing off trash cans and picnic tables.

Through a glaze of blood that now dripped in front of Katherine's eyes, she saw a very frail looking, old woman carrying several shopping bags suddenly appear on the grass not more than twenty feet away. The old crone with the long straggly gray hair, hooked nose, pointed chin and beady, green eyes stared at the vehicle hurtling towards her. She was far too old to move out of the way quickly enough. Katherine's screams seemed to awaken Christian's senses and he tried desperately to swerve the car to the right. It was too late to avoid hitting her, but at least it was not head on. Still, her fragile body was thrown up and onto the hood near the driver side fender, then struck the windshield with extreme force.

The old lady's bags were tossed into the air with all of her worldly belongings spraying in all directions. In what seemed like a sudden stopping of motion, Katherine looked through the broken windshield and could've sworn she saw an evil looking smile with yellow, rotted teeth upon the bag lady's face. Her body rolled off the hood of the car, dumped like her trash bags onto the park grass. The BMW now headed straight for a large oak tree near the edge of the pond.

The vehicle slammed into the tree at the corner of the right fender, sheering the entire side of the car completely off. Katherine sat stunned and exposed, but still strapped to the seat. Christian on the other hand had not been wearing his seat belt and as the car tilted violently to the left, he was thrown through the windshield towards the grass and the calm water of Long Pond.

The car now balanced precariously on the driver's side and slid slowly to a stop close to the water's edge. Even though the seat belt was still strapped tightly across her chest and shoulder, Katherine had slid somewhat and now hung suspended with the ground at her feet. Completely dazed and numb, she looked through the open, jagged windshield like it was a movie screen. She could see the ugly old crone lying in a heap on the grass, but struggling to sit up. Katherine also saw Christian's body, bent and bloody, Iying partially submerged in the water. It was a scene of pure insanity from a tragic movie running in slow motion.

The old hag raised her bloody face and pointed toward Christian who lay at the edge of the pond with only his head, right arm and shoulder out of the water. The noise of the crash had nearly deafened Katherine so all she could see was the old woman pointing towards her fiancée and mouthing some words that sounded like a chant.

Suddenly there was a bright burst of light above the water, temporarily blinding Katherine. At the same time her hearing seemed to return completely and she heard the breaking of glass. Glancing up she fearfully saw a large piece of what was left of the passenger door window break free and fall towards her. The very last thing she felt before being carried off to blessed oblivion was the edge of the glass slicing and tearing down the right side of her face. Then thankfully there was only darkness.

The coming weeks and months were nothing more than a blurred nightmare. It was a tortured period of pain and numbness, both physical and mental. Katherine found out later from her mother that she had been in the hospital for just shy of eight weeks. During much of that time, especially early on, she had been in a coma, some of which was medically induced by pain medication. There were several operations to not only repair a few broken bones, but suture together her badly lacerated face and scalp. She had mercifully stopped looking into a mirror because the ugly caricature staring back resembled nothing else but the bride of Frankenstein.

She also over the coming months became aware of what had taken place, especially after she had blacked out. The old woman had surprisingly survived her extensive injuries, but after a few weeks of being hospitalized she disappeared one night to the chagrin of a confused medical staff. However, the surprising and mysterious part of the whole story still caused everybody, law enforcement in particular, to scratch their heads in disbelief.

Katherine had not been much help to them other than flashing moments of memory. Christian lying nearly submerged in the water, the old crone lifting her arm and uttering some words that could not be heard clearly, a blinding flash of light before the broken glass tore down the side of her face and carried her away to an ongoing nightmare.

From what her mother revealed, Christian's body was never found. The police had spent days dredging the pond along with the aid of divers, but to no avail. It was as if he had vanished into thin air and nobody could explain why, especially since the old woman had disappeared as well. All that was found in the pond were fish and a surprising number of croaking frogs.

Now exactly one year later Katherine sat against the same oak tree which Christian's BMW had so violently struck. She stared across the smooth water of Long Acre Pond feeling emotionless, drained of her spirit with so many questions remaining unanswered. The most important question of all was still what had happened to Christian's body?

A sudden sound brought her out of the trance she had fallen into. She unconsciously touched the ugly scar on the side of her face as it immediately began to tingle like it was alive. She had already been through two surgical attempts to remove the scar and regain some semblance of a normal life. But when the bandages were removed, the grotesque scar remained, leaving the surgeons completely baffled. She had refused a third attempt, realizing that it was some type of curse.

The sound appeared again and she noticed that a large frog had come to the water's edge and now sat with fat body spread on a flat, smooth rock. It croaked softly several times and then moved off the rock and onto the grass a few feet closer to her.

Katherine attempted to smile and then quickly stopped because the scar seemed to suddenly burn.

"So Mr. Frog, can you tell me what happened one year ago today? Do you know where my Christian disappeared to? Are you in fact my Prince Charming?"

Nothing! Silence! Then a 'ribbit' and the frog with the large, black, bulging eyes jumped closer, almost to her feet.

Katherine sighed and chuckled softly. "Well, even if you knew what happened, how could you tell me? Oh why do I continue to torture myself so much about this? What's done is done and my life has sunken to where I now talk to frogs hoping for answers. I am so pathetic, physically and emotionally."

She began to rise and then was startled when the frog leaped upon her skirt, several loud 'ribbits' making it appear like the small green creature was actually trying to keep her from leaving and surprisingly trying to say something.

Katherine stared at the frog in amazement. "Well, this is not only confusing, but somewhat comical, though smiling for me is absolutely out of the question. But maybe you can smile, is that possible?"

Silence, then three more 'ribbits' as the frog moved even closer up her lap.

"Wait a minute, what's going on here?" Katherine inquired. "My life has been a nightmare this past year. Now suddenly it seems like a dream, a stupid fairy tale. So am I supposed to kiss you? Why in the world would you want somebody as ugly as me to kiss you?"

ribbit...ribbit...ribbit!

"Well, I suppose it wouldn't hurt since nobody else has asked for a kiss recently. Oh come here," she said, turning over both hands with palms up.

The frog leaped onto her hands and she was surprised at how heavy it was. She brought the frog slowly up to her face and prayed that nobody in the park was looking her way.

"Alright Mr. Frog, Prince 'whatever your name is', please allow me to try and put a smile on your lips."

She brought the small creature forward and kissed it on top of the head instead, not wanting to risk the frog sticking out a long, flickering tongue at the same time. That would be carrying this charade a little too far, not to escape the fact it would be rather disgusting. After all, just kissing the frog anywhere should be enough she felt.

However, whether it was a charade or a dream, a shower of yellow sparkles and bright light appeared. It temporarily blinded her, almost painfully, yet covered her in a soft blanket of pearly white mist. Katherine felt warm and tingly, like little bursts of electrical current were racing across her skin and through her veins.

When the tingling stopped she realized her eyes had been tightly closed so she slowly opened them. Her hands were still spread, palms facing the sky, but the frog was gone and only the placid pond was in front of her.

"Strange, very strange," she murmured. "This is all way too weird, but it seems that again there is a disappearance."

"I agree, very strange and very weird," appeared a strong, masculine voice behind her. "Hello Kate."

Startled, she leaped to her feet and spun quickly around. In a state of shock, Katherine began backing up towards the water's edge.

"Be careful Katie, you'll fall back into the water," Christian said softly, not wanting to frighten her more than she was, extending a hand towards her.

"It's not possible," she muttered, "This is a dream, more of my nightmare. It's just not fair. How can this be Chris? Where have you been all this time? I thought you were dead; your body had disappeared."

He smiled and chuckled softly, a sound she had not heard in so long.

"You wouldn't believe me right now even if I told you Katherine," he replied. "But, I'm back now and it was your kiss, those sweet lips that made it happen. I've missed you terribly and love you so much.

She backed away, her right hand covering the scar on her cheek.

"No, please go away Christian. I'm ugly, deformed. No man could ever want me again," she said, tears streaming down her face.

He moved quickly, putting his strong hands on her shoulders. She thought he was so handsome standing there in what appeared to be the very same clothes he had been wearing the day of the accident.

"My dearest Katherine, you are as exquisitely beautiful now as the first day we met. I've missed you terribly."

"No, you're just saying that because you don't want to hurt me. This cursed scar is ugly and I should leave. Please release me Christian and let me go. Find happiness with someone else," she pleaded tearfully, struggling to get free of his firm, but soft, grip.

"What scar? My dear Katherine, look down into the water. Sweetheart, there is no scar. You are as radiantly beautiful today as you always were."

She glanced down and saw her reflection staring back with smooth and flawless skin, her cheek devoid of ugliness. It was her face before that tragic day.

Katherine looked up at his handsome face and smiled beautifully. "How is this possible? I haven't smiled in a year."

He lovingly stroked the smoothness of her right cheek. "Believe me, I haven't smiled either. Some things are just unexplainable. Whatever happened was apparently because of the old lady I hit that day. I have so missed your smile and I'm so deeply sorry for the pain I've caused you. Can you ever forgive me?"

Holding his hand tightly they walked away from the pond. Placing her head against his chest she sighed heavily, a sigh of pure contentment.

"I thought I would never find happiness again and had begun to realize that possibly only frogs could smile. Of course I forgive you Christian, I love you so much," she said softly.

He squeezed her shoulders and kissed the top of her forehead which was also now free of the nasty looking scar which she hid beneath her bangs.

"Well my dearest Katherine, you at least made one very lucky frog smile today, that's for sure," he replied.

As they strolled away from the pond, locked tightly together arm in arm, the only sound in the air beside that of chirping song birds and the beat of their own hearts was the symphony of croaking frogs.

Across the park, on the other side of the pond, behind some trees stared two small, beady green eyes set above the flash of yellow, rotted teeth. The old woman smiled and moved forward toting her large bags for it was time to feed the frogs again...ribbit... ribbit

THE END

IN THE SHADOW OF A BEAST

(Based upon my poem within this book of the same name)

As my fingertips angrily struck the keys I could see the strangest of shadows dancing across the bookshelf to my right. It seemed to oddly resemble a very long, narrow hand, somewhat other than human, possessing sharp claws where fingernails should've rightfully been. It's quite ironic how the mind can play deranged games with one's incredible imagination, especially when that person has not slept in nearly forty-eight hours. Existing on nothing but large mugs of very strong black coffee and surfing upon waves of insomnia that would not allow me to sleep I continued to pound away at the keyboard hour after interminable hour. There was just an insane, driving force to finish this latest novel. In fact, I had never in my life poured out the words so fast, or written in such graphic, terrifying detail. However, what frightened me the most was the nagging feeling that I was not alone in creating this nightmarish tale. I shuddered to think who I was collaborating with.

I was also completely aware without even opening the front door to the porch and staring up at the nighttime sky that a full moon hung high. The persistent itching underneath my skin, like I was being devoured on the inside by marauding termites, clearly heralded the moon's call to me. Just like last month and the month before. Muscles throughout my body had begun humming so loud it became unbearable, to the point where at times I covered my ears with shaking hands. Quite frankly it didn't help because the noise was coming from within, a symphonic crescendo building towards a deafening clash of cymbals and kettle drums.

Suddenly a sharp, stabbing pain pierced my stomach and shot like a hot flame up my spine. I cried out in anguish, bending over towards the desk, my hands and fingers clutching for keys that weren't there, curling into what resembled the paws of some wretched beast. The tips of claws broke through the skin of my fingers and began to extend outward, curving at the ends and scratching at the keyboard, as if the beast wanted to type a bloody, monstrous paragraph.

Through what lost shreds of humanity I still precariously clung to, I recalled that horrendous night three or four months ago. Maybe longer, possibly shorter, I couldn't tell anymore because time simply was not what it used to be. As my heels clicked briskly along the lonely sidewalk edging the northern side of Rittenhouse Square I was rather somewhat apprehensive and more than a little nervous. Fortunately enough I had found a parking place relatively close to the bar where I had met several close friends for a late dinner and cocktails.

However, the stark headlines from the Philadelphia Inquirer over the past few months still cried out to me and other Philadelphians with stories of savage murders occurring, mostly around the full moon. I glanced up to see that big yellow orb suspended right above me. I swallowed hard and grasped the strap of my purse tighter. Looking at my watch I took note that it was nearly midnight. Picking up the pace and getting to the car in one piece was now my only desire. In my nervous hand, perspiring even on this frigid evening, was clutched a canister of mace and I would not hesitate in the least to use it. I might not be the most aggressive individual, but if my life was in extreme danger I would fight like a hellcat. If I was fast enough that is.

But I wasn't! Whatever the devilish creature was that sprung from the bushes, it hurtled towards me with blinding speed. The roar was totally deafening and I screamed loud enough to wake the dead. I don't know which was louder, but it didn't matter as the beast struck my side, violently slamming me to the pavement. I felt razor sharp claws rake my left shoulder and fangs that should not have belonged to any living creature sink deeply into my right arm. The pain was immediate and intense, but I was actually more stunned with the suddenness of the attack. I pushed and struggled as best I could against the massive weight that seemed to be crushing the air from my lungs. I was unable to scream for lack of oxygen, so I gasped and whimpered with what breath remained. I felt that in seconds I would be dead anyway.

And then, as fast as it had started, it ended just as abruptly. The monstrous body covered with stinking, matted fur and possessing wretched, fetid breath that had pounced upon me so savagely was suddenly gone. Its' roar and my screams still echoed against high-rise buildings sur-rounding the square as I lay sprawled on the sidewalk, dazed and fighting desperately to hold onto sanity. Several streams of blood flowed from my shoulder and arm, staining the white pavement red.

After two days in the hospital, the doctor signed me out expressing some medical disbelief that I could heal so quickly. I couldn't explain it either because I had seen the ugly wounds on my body and was extremely worried about infections and rabies. Yet even while I was lying in the emergency room the pain miraculously began to disappear. The police questioned me while I floated in and out of consciousness. They stared at me with raised eyebrows as if my story was preposterous.

A monster indeed! They said it must have been a very large dog, but I knew otherwise. Unless this mutt came straight from Hell, it was much more powerful and vicious than any old domestic fido could've been. Smiling, I thought of a gigantic poodle with slobbering fangs and murderous claws.

However, now my fractured life had become cruelly ruled by a cycle of full moons that coincidentally appeared about every 29.5 days. The closer it got to D-Day, the more anxious and paranoid I became. It wasn't the form of anxiety that I longed for either, as if you were waiting impatiently for a hot lover to come into your arms.

Oh no, this was more like a storm of insidious fear, the type of which I had never experienced before. Added to the fact that I clearly lost any memory of what happened on those frightful nights. The pain, the terror, the deep urgency from which the moon's clutches enveloped me pushed any threads of sanity to the farthest and darkest edges of my once normal existence. Any semblance of humanity disappeared completely and was evilly replaced by the sinister, voracious, feral mind of a wild and uncontrollable beast.

More pain pierced and jabbed at my bones and muscles, skin seeming to be ripped apart like paper-mache'. What I feared the most was hidden underneath. In a gut-wrenching jolt my spine cracked and bent, popping loudly as the vertebrae altered to where it was no longer human in form. I lifted my head towards the ceiling and moaned, or whined, not actually sure what came out. Sounds were no longer what I remembered them as being for my ears seemed longer now, much more sensitive and alert to danger, as well as prey. I could hear the terrified heart-beats of little animals and sensed their sweet, delicious fear.

I opened my eyes only to strangely gaze through varied shades of gray with intermittent flashes of brilliant color. What I saw sent icy chills up and down my altering spine. Fingertips of shadow slithered like a serpent over the keyboard, caressing the dark brown, wooden surface of the desk. Startled, I noted that they were elongated and sharp, like claws of a creature ~ the fanged and furry beast I write about ~ the beast that always has and will forever haunt my fractured dreams. It had been those dreams and imagination that created my stories.

Now, I wasn't quite so sure if it was that alone. Glancing through red, sleep-depraved eyes I saw long, red hairs upon my hands springing from every pore in my skin.

Through the pain and torment of shifting shape I tasted salty liquid upon my long, flickering tongue. I made a mewling sound as I realized it was tears, maybe all that was left of my humanity. Standing precariously upon bent legs I violently shoved the chair out from underneath me and glanced to my right. Now upon the bookshelf was the unmistakable shadow of a beast, possibly a wolf, its' muzzle long and narrow, ears somewhat rounded but coming to a point, curved fangs showing clearly as the mouth snapped open and closed.

The rear window in the den was open, a chilly evening air spilling into the room with a host of interesting sounds and tantalizing scents calling out to the beast. As the creature's paws alit upon the ground, the city streets of Philadelphia were soon filled with the howling of a wild and feral animal. Most individuals hearing the haunting lament from a distance swore it had to be a dog. And yet, it clearly sounded like a wolf, but they simply did not exist in the City of Brotherly Love. At least, that's what any normal person would think. If they were too close to the howling, then they could very well find out the hard way, staring up at the moon with disbelieving eyes.

At some point the next morning I awoke, stretching my painful limbs and moaning quite loudly. Blessed sleep had come at last, but at what expense? Strangely I found myself lying on the floor atop a round throw rug, a plush white robe tightly hugging my quivering body. Standing slowly, I began to stagger somewhat to the kitchen where I poured whatever coffee was left in the bottom of the pot into an unwashed mug from the kitchen sink. The coffee was cold, but I didn't care. I just needed caffeine and lots of it.

Wiping my mouth with the back of my hand, I shuffled to the front door and squinted as the light pierced deep behind my eyes. I quickly reached for the newspaper and rushed back inside the darker confines of the living room. Too frightened to actually look at the headlines yet, I moved slowly back to the kitchen in order to brew a large pot of coffee. As I listened to the steady percolating sound of the coffee machine, I glanced down at my feet where I saw blood splattered across the toes and ankles. Lifting my hands, I detected long red hairs still clinging to my skin and my nails were much longer and sharper than I remembered them being.

Moving to the farther wall I nervously stared into a small mirror. Opening my mouth, I glimpsed teeth that were not fangs, but still longer and sharper than normal for a human. Pain rolled through my stomach and I doubled over at the waist. This time though the agony was not from altering joints, but instead the sickening realization of what I possibly had become. Even more terrifying was what had I done in order to have blood on my feet and as I quickly noted other places as well? Before the pain subsided I was on my knees and retching uncontrollably into a trash can. I vomited until my stomach muscles were tied in knots and nothing else came out.

Standing slowly, teetering on very shaky legs, I staggered blindly into the living room where I had left the Inquirer. Fearing the worst, I spread the paper on the coffee table and stared, my eyes widening and a sobbing sound escaping my chest and parched throat.

Startled, horrified and utterly sickened, the headlines screamed at me: "Young Couple Slain in Fairmount Park. Witnesses swear they saw a large, wolf-like creature."

I placed my head in my hands and whispered, "Oh dear God, please forgive me for what sins I may have committed." Then I happened to glance at the corner of the newspaper and noticed that the date was from two days ago. I must've been unconscious for up to a full day, maybe more.

Tripping and stumbling towards the desk ~ seemingly my only safe haven~ I brought up the latest manuscript I had been writing. I waited with bitter disquietude, fearful of what I would see. Suddenly, the stark manuscript appeared and with a breaking heart I read of murder, death and mayhem in Fairmount Park. The title of the manuscript read "In the Shadow of a Beast".

Closing my eyelids to the burning realization that I could in fact be the creature responsible for these deaths, I began to shake and moan. I prayed that I would fall asleep and never awake, no more words of death to be typed or read ever again. But deep inside me was the voice of a wolf, a voracious monster. "Open your eyes and write about us, about me, about the urge to kill and run as the beast." The voice was low, guttural, seeming to come from inside me and yet not. I lifted my arms and let my fingertips begin striking the keyboard for I had a novel to finish.

Perhaps it would be completed before the next full moon. If not, then death would be the final chapter for within the feral eyes of the beast there is only one way—violence.

THE END

AMID THE SILENT LEAVES

Morning dawned with a sad malaise, typical fall day within Philadelphia. The street was awash in newly strewn leaves of dried yellows, painful reds, and jaded greens. Pulling the collar of my jacket around my neck I stepped off the porch into a swirling sea of color, shuffling my feet as I ambled along just as I would barefoot within the lapping shallows of the ocean's frothy edge.

Lost within a mood of deep regret, that bottomless pit of tears had been reached. There were no more. Ironic how a mood can match the weather, but then fall is for lovers holding hands, or those dejected grasping onto thoughts of sadness. Hearing my dog bark I saw her romping in a pile of leaves while a small, whirling dervish kicked them up into a tiny frenzy. Smiling, I realized how much I loved her, the daily devotion she showed me without condition, expecting absolutely nothing in return. Of course, she was spoiled rotten because I returned her unconditional love three fold. I would miss her greatly.

Breathing deeply, I wanted to remember the brisk freshness of the sea-son I enjoyed the most. Winter was so bone chilling cold even though I loved gazing romantically upon snowflakes swirling in soft virgin dance, whispering down to cleanse us of our lies, deceit, and anger. Summer was too damn hot and stifling, nasty when that perspiration trickled wildly down the small of your back. Spring was a nice, gentle interlude, rarely lasting long enough before the furnace winds of July began blowing. No, fall was clearly my special time of the year so it seemed more than appropriate for what was on my mind, the finality of it all.

"Come on sweetie pie, time to go in the house. You've scared all the monsters and night-time critters away again," I called to her, wondering if she would come right away since she most definitely had a stubborn streak that I would miss. "Come on baby, time for a treat." That always got her as she came bounding towards me.

With her large, fluffy tail fanning the brisk air she pranced across the yard to where I stood silently, words from the E-mail still ringing in my ears, etched forever upon my eyes. Another stiff breeze blew my long auburn hair across my face like tiny whips. It felt kind of good though, a form of self-flagellation, so I didn't bother pulling it back behind my ears which I normally would've done. The frantic dog reared up on her hind legs and grinned broadly, black and red spotted tongue from her chow-shepherd mixed breeding hanging out the front of her mouth. She was without a doubt the most beautiful and happy dog I had ever known. Several tears broke free, running haphazardly down a cold cheek, just another broken piece of my dreams and desires cascading away.

I always wondered about a broken heart, if it really was possible and how much pain there would be if it truly happened. At times during my life I certainly thought my heart had been broken. Now I knew that those episodes were mere dents or scratches, mending with time. The breakable heart was definitely the one exposed to a bone crushing agony, loss of desire and dreams, the emptiness that was all l consuming, a strangling realization that life now had absolutely no meaning, or purpose.

Inside the house I admonished her for being too loud as I gave her several treats she could happily munch away on. Staring down at the chair where my husband slept created a hollow emptiness, a guilt that I would carry with me, but no more than I had been living with for some time now. I remembered back to the day we had met thirty years ago when he jumped down from a tow truck clad in dirty coveralls, a train conductor's cap perched atop his handsome face. My car had broken down and there was my knight standing before me, grinning broadly, the furthest thing from riding a magnificent steed or clad in shining armor. His love was true and forever, while mine had become tarnished, lost in the shadows of a life devoid of happiness.

Wiping away tears I leaned down, kissed him gently on the cheek and whispered, "Good-bye, I do love you."

I glanced down at the computer screen, silently reading those painful words from the E-mail one last time. Seeing the finality of the expected, knowing that the deep love discovered two years ago amid a dream of happy days now lay dashed at my feet. It had become too painful suffering through another day.

It was a relationship that seemed doomed from the beginning and yet it was two hungry hearts so destined to meet. I tried to smile through the tears realizing that nobody in my entire life had ever made such an impact and it was easy to see that no one ever would again. From the instant our eyes met I was captivated. My heart was captured as a sacrifice to what love could truly be no matter how many obstacles had been placed in our path, or those who worked so diligently to destroy it.

Yet enough damage had been wrought. Too much pain, frayed nerves, and shattered feelings, not just our own, but for those around us as well. A tragic story of love experienced, fractured dreams forever lost, and the fantasy of two people meant to be as one, but to forever have this love forbidden. I was never strong enough to walk away, tied to a special person that comes along but once in a lifetime.

Staring at the words which ended my dream, I realized with a heavy heart now shattered within my chest, the final decision for me was an easy one. Walking towards the front door I knelt and held my loving dog that in the end would miss me the most for her love was truly the strongest and most honest of all. Reaching for the door knob I glanced back at my husband who was still asleep and whispered farewell.

On this quiet fall morning the sun tried to scratch through a thick cloud cover, but it could never slice through the heaviness within my heart. Many decisions are difficult ones, some cowardly and others brave, with a few that can change the lives of others. As I walked across the lonely street and let my leaden feet swish through a colorful, vibrant carpet of leaves, I knew my decision was final for a heart this broken could never again be mended.

Stopping at the top of a small hill I turned and glanced back, the house still in view. There were no tears left to fall now. They had all been shed with the pain inside me going from deep and intense, to dull and lifeless. In one pocket was a small brown bottle that contained my one-way ticket to another existence. I agonized over the sin I was about to commit, but for me the utmost sin would be going on and living a lie. Maybe others could, but once the fantasy had been caressed and then pulled away, the desire to continue in a world of lonely thoughts was too much to suffer through. I had felt the deepest love possible and nothing else could ever compare.

Glancing up at a solitary beam of sunlight breaking through a canopy of leafless tree limbs, I knelt and smiled. My thoughts were upon the one person who I would remember as I expelled my final breath. I had said so many times over the last two years that never would another individual control my heart and feelings so much. Falling softly to the ground, an empty bottle rolling from my open hand, I whispered "I love you" as words from a very special poem were the last ones I would ever hear.

"beneath these trees I quietly lie,
solitary and alone,
stark and brittle leaves of forgiveness
blowing to cover up such a deep sense of loss,
for eternal love has died as now have I,
free at last to fade away amid the silence of the leaves...."

Quietly the leaves swirled in a tragic dance, covering my lifeless body and hopefully transporting my soul to a special place where pain could no longer touch me.

In a house across the street a dog whimpered as a solid tear appeared in the corner of her eye. In another room a computerized voice broke the stillness. "You have mail."

Several days later one special message would read, "Hi honey, I'm so very sorry for hurting you. Would you please forgive me? I do love you so very, very much."

THE END

EDGES OF REALITY
MONSTROUS SHADOWS

The fog
lies thick and dense,
whispering in voices dark,
slithering with evil as blood drips to mix
with tears, deepening sense of dread.
What lies beyond our reality?
Edges torn and dead,
hope lost within
this fog.

When fog becomes so thick and dense you're barely able to see your quivering hand extended, is there an ending to it? As it swirls mysteriously like a serpent around your shivering body, lapping eerily against your startled face, might it just be deadly silence, or is that a perceptible hiss you hear, a faint crackle like a balled-up piece of plastic wrap slowly expanding to spring open like a wild flower in early morn?

If you chose the first option, then you're probably safe. Proceed slowly, just be very careful, extremely wary of unseen obstacles that could possibly injure or severely maim. However, the murderous hiss or crackling sound might possibly be an entirely different story altogether, perhaps that lurking nightmare which haunts the midnight hours. Perhaps you could just turn around and travel back the way you came if you knew what way that was, the fog being so thick now that any sense of direction is completely lost. Having spun around so many times already attempting to decide which way to travel, the entry point into this vast sea of cool, dense, haunting mist is long forgotten. Bravely you could simply plunge straight ahead, but then will this terrifying, electrically charged grayish morass ever end?

Or...at the edge of this ragged piece of reality might the flimsy fabric of what we knew to be, the stale breath of what once had been, the fragile existence which at one time could've been a footstep upon our lives...could this be another parallel where dreams are but nightmares and the edges of reality a portal which we dare not cross?

It is that for sure, but not in the way you may have first intended. Reality is only what we perceive it to be, yet possessing jagged cracks and deadly slashes to frightening depths unforeseen. In fact, as you struggle through such a threatening fog, then life as previously known may very well be lost forever.

A nightmare has been placed into motion, the likes of which one could never have imagined even after reading all those scary fairy tales of monsters, goblins, and green-eyed ogres as a wild-eyed child. Call it being in the wrong place at the wrong time, curiosity killed the cat, or as Euripides once said, 'No one can confidently say that he will still be living tomorrow'. We can only ponder what lies beyond the edges of our current perception. But be aware without a shadow of a doubt that the world is not always what it appears to be

The fog continues to slither across the ground and reach skyward blotting out any hope of sunlight, the rhythmic flow of clouds that mimic our breathing, a border between heaven and hell. It floats and dances as if it lives with a maniacal purpose. Unnatural, it issues a nightmarish hint that something sinister, or possibly a separate and demonic world, may actually border upon these edges of reality, lurking as terrifying evil within. It is tattered sanity ripped by bloody claws from creatures we dare not conjure up. Perhaps another existence that runs parallel to our own, a place where nightmares become reality, that intuition can be classified as bad luck, where good fortune is nothing more than a hovering death sentence. In other words, not a sunny, idealistic place you'd wish to find yourself for very long.

However, this is exactly the place where Jason Manning found himself, standing utterly still beside the smaller and curvier figure of Kimberly Miller. They both listened intently to the mysterious sounds twirling about them, no idea what they could be, or even from what direction they might be coming from. The hi-speed, ultra-expensive bikes they had been riding now lay broken and discarded after colliding with each other at the intersection of Shawmont and Umbria in the Roxborough section of Philadelphia.

As Jason sped around the sharp, right hand turn which he had maneuvered so many times before, he found himself suddenly immersed in a fog so thick he had no idea what lay ahead of him. It was both startling and terrifying. Sadly, what stood directly in his path was poor Kimberly who sat confused in a mental fog of her own upon her thin bicycle seat, too frightened to turn around and go back the way she had ridden. That is, if she knew what way that was, which she absolutely did not.

Jason's front tire smashed into the front of her bike in a clattering sound of metal. He flew over the handlebars, disappearing into the grayish murk. She fell heavily to the pavement with a loud thud beneath what remained of her broken bike. Not knowing who or what had struck her, she quickly realized that she was not badly hurt, just more stunned than anything. Grabbing the bike with her gloved hands she lifted and then pushed up with her feet to send the bike reeling into the dense fog in front of her.

Standing upright she started tenderly feeling her arms and legs. Nothing appeared to be broken thankfully although her right hip and the back of her head was slowly beginning to ache, not to mention a quick moment of dizziness. Kimberly then spun half way around when something that sounded like a painful moan appeared from the frightening morass behind her. She listened intently until the same moan came again, like a groan of obvious discomfort.

"Who's there? Are you hurt?" she inquired, her voice quivering, more a whisper than an actual verbal question, her throat completely dry with water bottle discarded where the broken bike now lay.

Mostly silence was her answer, just that damn hissing sound like a snake issuing a warning not to come any nearer. She took a tentative step forward anyway and then stopped, a pounding in her head nothing more than the frightened beating of her heart.

Slightly louder, she asked, "Where are you? I can't see a damn thing in this creepy stuff."

After a few seconds a low groan appeared and then a strained voice. "I think in front...of you. I seem...to be lying up...against the guard... rail."

"And where the hell is that? I have no idea where anything is right now," she inquired, voice bordering on the hysterical.

More silence, longer this time so she immediately became worried that he had passed out, or maybe even worse. Was she now alone? She took a few more uneven, shuffling steps forward and then quickly stopped.

"Hey...can you still hear me? Please tell me you can hear my voice," she spoke into a fog that pressed against her lips, voice strained nearly to the point of breaking.

"I'm okay...just come straight forward...I think I see your shadow."

Kimberly began inching ahead and then bravely took two longer strides, her right foot making contact with something soft.

"Ouch...damn...you stepped...on my ankle," Jason said, looking straight up as she stood over him. "I'm down here...on the ground."

She dropped her gaze to see his sprawled form through the swirling fog, bending quickly and then seeing him a little more clearly. Realizing he was lying at a most unnatural angle against the curb and guardrail, she reached forward as gently as possible and attempted to arrange him more into a somewhat comfortable resting position.

"Whoa...hold it, damn. ..okay, that's enough," he responded in a panting voice, acute pain in his left knee beginning to become much more prominent, reaching deep down behind the kneecap like it was about to be yanked out by some unseen hand.

"How badly are you hurt?" she inquired, obviously concerned and then moved back slightly. As she did so, however, the thought struck her that she was actually kneeling in what could possibly be the middle of a car lane on what was normally a busy Shawmont Avenue. This being early Sunday morning, traffic was thankfully sparse. She slid forward, praying that a car did not come careening out of nowhere to wipe her out before she had any chance to say good-bye to her loved ones.

"Christ, I'm not sure. My left knee is hurting really bad right now, I think it's bleeding, but I don't think it's broke," he answered, pulling his hand closer to his face and seeing that he was correct, his gloved fingers covered with blood.

Moving a little closer, she asked, "Do you want to try and stand up? I'm not sure this is the best place for either of us to be quite frankly."

Jason started pushing himself up with the aid of the guardrail. "You're probably right. Can you give me a hand?"

Kimberly gently grabbed his arm and then realized she needed to be more firm. Shortly he was standing as well, wincing in pain as he attempted to put pressure on his leg, but now standing nonetheless.

He reached for his waist and unsnapped the thin belt that held a water bottle and small, wallet-size leather pouch which held his ID, cell phone, and a little cash. Pulling the water bottle free he handed it to Kimberly who accepted it greedily. She was thirsty but knew she couldn't be a glutton, taking a few quick sips and then one more. Reaching down, Jason encircled his leg just above the knee with the belt, tugged tight so that it acted as a tourniquet, and then tried a few tentative steps. Not bad he thought, knowing he needed to stop the steady flow of blood till he at least got some medical attention.

"Feel okay?" she asked him, getting more nervous by the minute.

"Yeah, I think so. Christ, what a mess this is, huh?" Pausing slightly, he then asked, "I don't know your name, mine's Jason."

She laughed, trying not to allow the sharp concern to show. "Not really the way I would've chosen to meet you Jason, but what's done is done. My name is Kimberly, Kim for short. So you didn't see me sit-ting on the bike before you slammed into me?"

Maneuvering slightly, he chuckled. "Yeah right, as if you could see anything in this slop. So why did you stop in the middle of the road?"

"Hey, watch it buster. I was near the curb on the turn, not in the middle of the street...er, at least I thought I was."

Taking a few tiny steps, his lips pressed together in a grimace of pain, he replied, "I was just kidding Kím. I'm sorry I messed up your bike. Are you hurt at all?"

Reaching behind and rubbing her right hip, more towards the ass end, she reported, "Just my pride I think, though my head hit fairly hard. Thankfully I was still wearing my helmet. So what should we do now?"

Taking her arm and then placing a hand on her shoulder, he took another step forward, more like a shuffling jump. "I think there's a house across the street. I've ridden past this spot so many times I know there are a few homes along here. Unless my depth perception is so screwed up, we just need to get off this road. Are you ready?"

"Yeah, I guess so though quite frankly I'm really kind of scared. Hey, isn't that the house that belongs to some female police detective? I think she's the one that was attacked by some savage beast last year?"

He limped forward with the help of her arm to balance upon. "I'm not sure really, but there has been so many strange killings in this city over the last six months that I'd just about believe anything."

Holding onto each other, they took baby steps and shuffled across the pavement, completely unable to see their feet lost in the swirling fog below. The annoying hiss continued and was now accompanied by a low sound that, to Jason at least, appeared to possibly be a growl. Feeling the pressure of Kimberly's fingers on his arm, he knew that she heard it as well.

Suddenly her left foot struck something hard and with her momentum going forward she began reeling towards the ground. Trying to still keep hold of Jason's arm and fearful of losing contact with possibly the only other human being within this mess, Kim's body spun around as her grip was torn loose. Her back and head struck the sidewalk hard, air violently slammed out of her lungs. She gasped for precious oxygen.

The low growl Jason had heard a few seconds ago now had turned into something very menacing. Several sharp, loud barks followed the growls and then a reddish blur materialized in the fog. Lying on her back, still somewhat stunned at the surprising fall, Kim looked up to see the head of a snarling animal with teeth barred. She screamed and rolled to her right, at the same time raising her arms to protect her head and face.

Seeing the body of the dog erupt through the fog Jason struck out with both hands, hoping to make enough contact to propel the animal's momentum away from Kimberly. Neither impact happened as the dog let out a loud yelp and quickly disappeared back into the thick soup from which it had leaped. Jason glanced down and could make out Kim's body so he bent painfully to grab hold of her left arm. Tugging hard, he slid her body away off the sidewalk and back out onto the street. Trying to forget about the throbbing pain which now pounded against his knee, he lowered his body to the ground and pulled Kimberly towards him.

His heart was pounding so loud in his chest that he had completely forgotten about the angry dog. Apparently it was the large, reddish-brown mutt that lived in the house with the detective. Thankfully, a chain had stopped the beast's momentum and saved Kimberly from any possible injuries.

"What the hell was that?" she whispered softly, her voice so dry that it came out more like a croak.

With a nervous laugh, Jason replied, "That damn dog from the house you said the detective lives in, the one that barks at everybody who walks or rides by. Christ, we can be glad it was attached to that chain."

Kimberly had raised herself now to a rather unstable sitting position as she touched the back of her head, nearly at the same place she had bounced upon when her bike was slammed into. Rotating her neck slowly, she realized this was turning out to be a real nightmare of what had started out as a nice, promising Sunday morning ride.

"Are you able to stand up? We can't stay here in case some stupid driver attempts to maneuver through this crap," he asked.

"Sure, I think so. My heart is still pounding inside my chest, but I'm not hurt. Damn dog scared the hell out of me. Better take my arm. You look ready to fall over."

Quickly standing, they held onto each other again, like desperately hugging life vests in a broiling sea. Backing slowly away from the sidewalk their eyes continued to squint as they stared ahead in case the dog had broken free. The sharp barking continued and echoed within the fog, making it sound like a pack of dogs were wildly yapping. Stopping suddenly, Kimberly glanced towards Jason.

"Which way do we go? Somehow we have to get out of this before we get hurt a lot more than we are now," she asked, adding a nervous chuckle at the end.

There was a pause before Jason answered. "The fog has to be just lying low in this valley and the house is still in front of us. That would mean if we turn right and start walking in that direction, then we'll be heading up hill hopefully to where the edge of this damn stuff starts to break up."

Just then he groaned in pain as he put too much pressure on his injured knee.

Kim held on tight. "Come on Jason, we can do this. Hey, didn't I see a cell phone in your pack when you put the belt around your leg?"

Jason moaned again, this time not in pain. "Yeah, damn it, I think I left the pack on the pavement when you helped me up and we moved forward. We need to go back to the railing and then feel around on the ground until we find it."

They turned slowly until they felt certain that if they walked forward they would eventually slam into the guardrail, or the curb. It took about a minute but they did just that, hitting the curb first and then falling into the railing like a couple of Keystone Kops. Jason swore an oath as his knee hit something before he squatted toward the pavement.

"You stay here, I'll start moving my hands over the street until I find it," Kimberly ordered, trying to sound brave, but not succeeding very well.

It actually didn't take long to find as she made a gleeful exclamation of triumph. She leaned behind her, grabbed the guardrail and started walking towards Jason.

"I found it, am I near you?"

"You're practically right on top of me neighbor," he joked in reply.

Seeing her body materialize through this cloud that hugged the earth, he reached for the phone and flipped it open. The green light on the screen looked strange and surreal within the fog. Thinking of Todd, his normal biking buddy with the exception of today, he dialed the number and held the phone to his ear.

There was nothing, no dial tone at all. It was deader than a doornail. Flipping the phone closed in disgust and grabbing it tightly like he wanted to squeeze the life out of it, he leaned his back against the rail and sighed.

"We couldn't be that lucky I guess. Phone's dead, nothing at all, "he told Kim.

"That's great!! What the hell is this stuff? It seems to be more than just some normal fog bank," she replied, rubbing the back of her hand across her eyes which suddenly appeared wet, either from tears or thick humidity that glistened upon her face.

"I don't know Kim, but let's go, we need to get out of whatever it is," he replied.

They both stood with the aid of each other and turned to the right, which meant they would be heading up hill. If Jason's memory served him correctly, there were four other hõuses on the left and nothing but a steep hill to the right covered with trees. This led to a curve in the road to the right and then there would be another straight away until a slight turn to the left. He prayed they wouldn't have to go too far before finding the edge of this sea of unearthly whiteness.

Moving slowly, but steadily, they suddenly stopped when another ominous growl appeared from the fog. This sound was definitely not the dog for it resonated deeper and was far more menacing. Jason felt a chill of fright race up and down his spine.

"What the hell is that?" Kimberly whispered, holding onto his left arm so tight that he began to wince.

"Lord only knows, but you have to stop squeezing my arm or it's going to go numb," he replied in a whisper of his own.

The sound was coming closer it seemed, the deep growls interspersed with loud grunts. Jason knew it was some type of animal for sure, but what the hell could it be? Unless it was a really huge dog, he sure as hell didn't want to find out, but felt that was going to be inevitable. Terrifying murders had been going on for months now in Philly.

Moving quickly to his right, even though he still couldn't see more than a few feet in front of him, he knelt on his good knee and reached off the road searching for anything he might use as a weapon. After a few seconds his hand touched what appeared to be a thick log. Grabbing it tightly he pulled and found it to be about three feet long. Standing up and suppressing a groan of pain he positioned himself somewhat ín front of Kimberly and held the log in both hands.

"Not sure if this will do any good, but if whatever's out there comes at us, I'll swing as hard as I can and you just run. Get the hell away from whatever it is."

"I won't leave you Jason, we're in this together," she replied with false bravado.

"Kim, don't be stupid," he hissed back. "One of us has to get out of this crap."

Just then a loud roar erupted from the fog as Jason saw a huge shadowy form coming straight towards them. Holy shit, he thought, this was sure as hell not the bike ride he had in mind when he left his center city townhouse this morning on his normally enjoyable weekend trek to Valley Forge National Park.

"Kimberly, get down," he yelled, raising the log and preparing for the concussion with some huge beast-like figure rushing dangerously in their direction.

When it was no more than about three feet away from Jason the fog seemed to swirl away from pressure of the oncoming huge body. He stared wide-eyed at the immense head of some monstrous wolf-like beast. The creature stood nearly seven feet tall on two legs as it roared again and swung, a terrifying hand towards Jason, long three-inch claws at the end of each finger.

Realizing that he was going to die, he got the courage to just swing the log as hard as he could like he was batting cleanup for his college baseball team. If he was going to die, then he definitely was going to give the beast something to remember him by. The log struck the massively furred arm with å loud thud. It also broke with an equally loud crack. But the blow was enough to stop the wolfish monster for a few seconds anyway, enough for Jason to move backwards as fast as he could scramble on one good leg.

Kim was slightly behind him, more frightened than she had ever been in her life. Their legs got entangled and they started to fall. As they did, there was a large reddish blur to their left, accompanied by another loud growl, but not from the monster.

Jason was able to see the dog from down the street hurtling towards the creature, two feet of chain still hanging from its collar.

Monster and dog collided with each other, the momentum from the flying canine catapulting both animals backwards into the fog. Jason and Kimberly were now sprawled on the pavement. They began to scramble like crabs to their left toward hopefully the other side of the road. From the fog came sounds of a frightening battle, but with the size of that beast, Jason didn't hold out much hope for the brave, but somewhat stupid, dog.

Suddenly the noise stopped and there was utter silence.

"What do we do?" Kim whispered next to his face. "Whatever the hell that beast was, that poor dog didn't have a chance even as brave as it was."

"You're asking me what to do? At this point, all we can hope for is that the dog was powerful enough to kill that creature or scare it off," he whispered back. "Otherwise we're dead for sure."

They crouched and waited for about a minute and still heard no sounds.

"Come on, we have to keep climbing up this hill. I can see a little further now so I'm hoping we're close to coming out of it," he said, grabbing her hand tightly.

All they could do was shuffle one foot in front of the other and pray that they weren't attacked. Jason wasn't sure what had happened, but the wolf-beast or the dog, had disappeared at least for the moment.

But it seemed that they couldn't be lucky enough to escape danger for the fog they found themselves immersed in was not anything this world normally was used to. As they struggled forward a loud, deafening screech crashed through the air behind them. Jason and Kimberly stopped, placing shaking hands over their ears. The screeching stopped and was then replaced with a loud flapping noise, like the sound of huge wings fracturing the air.

The two frightened bikers turned just in time to see a horrifying creature flying through the fog directly towards them. The face was almost human, but ugly as a bat out of hell. The wing span stretched four feet on both sides of a thick, muscular body. Two legs hung down with huge claws that reached for Kimberly as it whooshed forward.

"Get down," Jason yelled loudly, attempting to propel himself between her and the flying beast.

However, the right wing slapped him on the side with enough force to knock him painfully to the left, stunned from the severe concussion. Before he struck the ground and became lost completely in the fog, Jason saw the terrifying claws sink into Kimberly's shoulder and back.

Continuing to flap the huge wings, the creature rose into the thick mist clutching tightly to its struggling human prey. Her screams echoed through the fog as Jason landed hard on the ground, rolling over several times until he came to a slamming stop against the curb.

He wasn't sure how long he remained unconscious, could've been seconds, minutes, or an hour. Voices were coming from someplace, but he couldn't make out anything that made sense. Not sure if he wanted to open his eyes, all he could remember was some hairy creature and flying beast. Had it been some form of horrible nightmare? Then he remembered Kimberly and his eyes flew open in panic.

"Hey, are you okay?" came a strange voice from above and behind him. "Don't move in case you have any broken bones or internal injuries."

He moved anyway, the hell with the voice from whomever it was coming from.

"Did you see it?" he asked in a loud, hysterical voice. "The creature, did you see it flying away into the fog?"

"Alright sir, just lie down and relax, I think you've had some kind of nasty head injury," came another voice.

Jason glanced up and saw the figure of a man dressed in a police uniform.

"I'm okay damn it," Jason shot back, "the fog...there was this monstrous bird-thing that grabbed hold of Kimberly and flew away."

Silence filled the air. "Sorry buddy, there was no fog, no flying creatures, no maiden being carried away into the air. Were you hit by a car? Where's your bike?"

Suddenly a large red dog appeared from the trees behind where Jason lay with what appeared to be blood on its fur. It came up and began licking his face.

"Is this your dog?" questioned the cop. "It seems to me that you were riding a bike and crashed down the hill somewhere."

Pushing the dog away, Jason sat up. "Not mine, it's from the house down at the bottom of the hill. It broke loose from a chain and attacked some monstrous wolf thing that was attacking us."

"Okay, now listen, I thought you said it was some beast flying in the air?" asked the cop, his voice bordering on a laugh. "This is Philadelphia, not the jungle."

"The wolf attacked us lower down the hill in the fog. That dog stopped the creature and we continued climbing up the hill hoping to break clear. Then this flying thing came soaring through the air and grabbed Kimberly, took her away," Jason said, his voice rising and then falling away.

"So where is this Kimberly anyway? Were you riding together and both crashed?" asked the officer.

Angry, Jason pushed away and started to stand on his own. "Haven't you been listening to me?' I told you that she was carried away, you have to save her."

Just then a siren came from up the hill. Jason glanced to his right and saw the flashing light of an ambulance approaching them.

"Look officer, we need to find Kimberly before it's too late, if it isn't already," Jason said, his voice nearing the breaking point.

"We'll find her sir, don't worry. For now, you need to go to the hospital and get those injuries taken care of. Do you have any ID?"

Jason reached for the small pack that had been on his belt, but it wasn't there. "Christ, my ID is with my cell phone. There should be a small, black pouch lying on the road someplace. My name is Jason Manning. Her name is Kimberly, but I never got her last name."

"Okay, just relax, we'll find it and search for her. Now, I need you to let me help you over to the ambulance," the officer said, helping Jason limp towards the vehicle.

After lying down on the stretcher, Jason grabbed hold of the police officer's hand and squeezed tight. "Please, you have to find her, she might be dead already," Jason hissed loudly. "The creature flew into the fog and disappeared. I blacked out and didn't see exactly what direction it went.'

"Okay Mr. Manning, I promise, we'll find her," the cop replied, attempting to hide his disbelief. "I'll see you down at the hospital and get a full statement."

A few minutes later the ambulance turned around and roared back up the hill towards Ridge Avenue, lights flashing and siren blaring. Off to the side of the road sat the large red dog staring at the rear of the emergency vehicle and then glanced warily towards the other side of the road. She stood, turned and started trotting down the hill with her head continuing to stare at the woods on the other side of the street.

Officer Jennings turned around also as a squad car came to a stop beside him. "Hey Mike, find anything down there?"

"Yeah, two bikes pretty mangled at the bottom of the hill. We found this small black pouch with a cell phone, some money and ID for a Jason Manning. Inside another pack attached to the handlebars of the other bike was the ID for a Kimberly Miller. Did the ambulance take both of them away?"

Jennings stood and turned towards the woods as he heard a very loud screech from some type of large bird. "No, you wouldn't believe what that guy was ranting on and on about, but I do think something terrible has happened. Call the precinct and get more help out here. Oh, was it foggy down here this morning?"

"Not at all, I drove up Shawmont not more than an hour ago and it was fine."

"Yeah, I thought so," Officer Jennings mumbled, walking over to the sidewalk and then stared nervously into the thick, ominous woods.

Another loud screech and then he swore that something large moved away high up in the tree line. Actually, he wasn't really sure of anything now, just that his eyesight only went so far. It appeared that whatever lurked menacingly at the edge of his vision was something he couldn't be certain of. Scratching his head, he wondered what terrible occurrence had really happened on Shawmont Avenue, fog or not.

But then, as Jason Manning and Kimberly Miller had tragically come to discover, those fragmented edges of our reality may never truly appear what they seem to be, especially since monsters and living shadows did surely exist outside of nightmares.

THE END

SOMETHING'S WATCHING

A strong breeze angrily pushed the curtains away from the open window, white cotton fabric billowing and dancing in a ghostly soiree. Light from a resplendent full moon dressed the floor and bottom of my bed in a silver glow.

I lay there quietly, head and shoulders pushing back against two propped-up, over-stuffed pillows. Sleep had come early, mostly because of my weakened condition and a few greedily swallowed pills to aid that process. Now however, I was completely awake, waiting for the whisper to once again slither inside my head.

Life had not been the same since it first graced my ears, whispering, "Jennaaaleee...," that soft, deep, haunting voice stretching out my name in a sensual allure. It was impossible not to be drawn towards the moon's power. Bursting in full blown intensity, my willpower was totally lost. But, I knew clearly it was not the lunar factor alone for the moon couldn't whisper inside my brain, even if there truly was a little old man who lived there. Only a human was able to accomplish that feat, or at least something resembling a human. That was a realization I had trouble grasping hold of for I knew by now the source.

I lay there in the dark trying to remember when it had all began. Near as I could tell it was almost exactly one year ago. Curiously enough, that happened to be on the night of a full moon when I was returning from a birthday party for one of my nephews. It's true that I was a little tipsy because a few of us had decided to head for a corner bar after cake and ice cream. Not generally a beer drinker per se, those frozen mugs of Fosters went down much too smooth.

Strolling nonchalantly along the sidewalk, albeit upon unsteady legs, towards where I had left my car parked, I had to pass a small park with a low slung hill rising to an open area between two large, sentinel-like trees. The moon in all her glory hung suspended, framed by the massive limbs.

Gazing somewhat awestruck at the scene, I released a startled gasp for standing in front of the moon's surface was the tall, imposing figure of a man. He didn't move, but I could feel his intense glare resting directly upon me. For some unknown reason I also detected an ominous threat, a frightened nervousness like I was in the presence of something beastly, possibly evil.

Accelerating my pace, I made a bee-line straight for my car parked about a hundred feet away. Yet, I was unable to pull my gaze from this strange figure silhouetted in that lunar glow.

My name is Jennalee Parker. I'm nothing special, not rich by any standards, attractive to a point though definitely flawed in certain areas. I earn a fare wage for working hard all day on a computer. What I love to do is workout, jog and bike, so for that I'm physically in great shape. I need to workout because I also love to eat. Why some perverted molester would want me, I hadn't the foggiest idea.

The whisper appeared in my head as I neared the car. It drew out my name in a long, low, hissing sound. Heart pounding frantically inside my chest I fumbled for my keys, dropping them to the pavement. I knelt and clutched them between trembling fingers. Never once did I release my stare from the stranger upon the naked hill who had not moved even a fraction of an inch. I'm not certain why, but there was something animalistic to the scene, like predator versus prey. It was easy to figure out which one I was, not something I would give into easily though because I would fight tooth and nail.

The irritating whisper continued to echo in my head, " Jennaaaleee... come to meeee...."

Yanking open the car door I slipped inside and once again my handful of thumbs had trouble inserting the key into the ignition. I was so terrified at this point that calming down was impossible until I reached safety.

Suddenly, there was a roar all around me. Was it thunder, or the beast? Neither really! It was the pounding of my heart and the engine growling to life. Throwing the car into gear I pressed the accelerator hard and banged into the car behind me. Not taking the time to put my seat belt on l lurched forward, chin striking the steering wheel hard enough to make me cuss very unladylike. I quickly realized I was doing more harm to myself than apparently any creature could do at the moment.

Feeling guilty about not being able to leave any insurance info for the driver of the other car, I yanked the transmission into drive, frantically spun the steering wheel to the left, and then tromped down on the gas pedal. The car shot forward, right fender slamming into the vehicle parked in front of me. Didn't matter at this point, I would've driven through a brick wall to get away. Straightening out the trajectory, my Honda Civic hurtled forward and I could only hope there were no other cars in my way.

Speeding down the street I glanced in the rear view mirror only to see that the dark stranger had miraculously moved to stand in the middle of my lane. How the hell did he do that so fast I wondered?

The whisper continued, only louder and more urgent. "Jennaaaleee, come back to meeee....'

Yeah, like that was going to happen. Reaching the intersection and deciding not to stop, I glanced in the mirror one last time only to see that tall, dark, man-like figure turning into some type of crouching beast. Fear tore at my nerves while tremors shook my entire body.

That was twelve months ago and each month since then upon the full moon that whisper and dangerous apparition returned, mostly outside my window. Yet it wasn't really an apparition, it was very much reality. I know that for a fact because the second month he came to me again, either in a realistic dream or not, I couldn't tell for sure.

He was tall and broad shouldered, yet very trim around the waist. There was this quiet, confident, brooding aura about him. To say he was handsome would be a gross understatement for his rugged, chiseled face and masculinity stole my breath away. Staring at him through the window, he stood in the yard and raised his arms, beckoning and enticing me forward.

"Come to meeee, Jennaaaleee...," he mouthed silently, while the words echoed within my brain.

I really had absolutely no choice in the matter. Like a fish drawn towards a glittering, dancing lure, his voice and eyes drew me. He was the predator and I certainly was his prize catch apparently. Once outside beneath the moonlight I moved to stand no more than two feet away. His height and size dwarfed me. For some strange reason though, I was not frightened at that moment. So, besides his mesmerizing allure, he must've also cast some type of spell. How else could I explain the fact that I didn't bolt like a scared jack rabbit? Yet, the trance was in his words, that deep resonance to his voice, the strength in his hands and arms, that beastly yellow glow from his eyes. Hell, I was captivated and no longer my own person.

We had sex that night right there beneath the moonlight. I say sex because I didn't know him long enough for it to be true love and in my mind it never would be. Thankfully, it was in the backyard so at least there was no obvious spectacle for my nosy neighbors. He also strangely nibbled at my neck, seeming to draw blood, especially when I felt his tongue lapping against my skin.

"Are you some kind of bloodsucking vampire? Am I going to die tonight?"

He laughed in that low, breath-taking voice. "No, I am a creature of the night, but as alive as you are now and will continue to live for hopefully a very long time."

"Good for you," I replied. "Then why did you take my blood?"

"Simply because not only do I taketh, but you receiveth as well," he chuckled. "For now you need not know why, nor should you be afraid. I will not harm you."

"So, why pick me? I'm certainly nothing special, at least for someone like you."

He suddenly grasped my shoulders firmly and drew me forcefully into his massive embrace.

Whispering into my hair, he replied, "Because my sweet Jennalee, you are more special than you could ever imagine. You were chosen long ago, but had to come of age. Please believe me when I say that I've always been nearby making certain that you were never in any danger. Trust me for your life will never again be the same. Do not fear though for I will always be at your side."

I fell asleep that night wondering if it was all real and if I was now ensnared within his web, enslaved to this wildly magnetic, but dangerous, individual.

The next full moon he returned so I realized it was about as real as anything could ever get. Quite frankly, I was absolutely terrified. However, that did not diminish the intense, raw sex which was passionate, torrid, so steamy and at times angry, very nearly beastly. And yet, I yearned for more and he was always willing to supply what I wanted.

My shock came when we climaxed for the last time. I shut my eyes and screamed with an intensity never felt before. Even the ripping pain now experienced upon my arms and legs felt erotic.

But, when I opened my eyes I gasped in fear, completely stunned and amazed. Not more than six inches from my face was the massive head of a huge wolf, golden eyes blazing in desire, black lips pulled back in a feral grin. The beast's fangs dripped blood, as did his claws, thus the reason for the pain in my limbs.

This creature which I had never seen before leaped from the bed, turned to gaze at me with an intense desire before jumping through the open window. Seconds later the night resonated with a long, haunting, and very contented howl. Tears began streaming down my cheeks as I began to shake uncontrollably. Falling into a troubled sleep I had vivid nightmares about being ripped apart by a huge, grayish/black wolf.

Now, upon this magical evening, I lay awake, fully aware that the moon shown down brightly. It was once again his night and the wild scent of his body swam upon the breeze. I knew he was outside the window and always awaited my invitation. The beast was certainly polite for sure.

Oh, did I also mention I was pregnant? So, not only had my life been completely altered like he had changed from man to animal on more than one occasion, I inwardly feared what I now carried inside my womb. Placing my hands gently upon my stomach, I could feel that whatever was inside me happened to be very restless and active tonight, as if it wanted out. But, he was a man who was a wolf, so what could that portend?

When I glanced up, Dominik was standing by the window. Good Lord, he was stunningly handsome, breathtakingly so.

"You frighten me when you do that," I mumbled.

"Do what my dear?"

"When you appear so suddenly like that out of nowhere. Hey, did you just come in here on your own?"

He smiled and my heart fluttered. "You always invite me in dear Jenna, even if it's simply a thought which I can always hear. How do you feel tonight?"

Gazing at his perfect face and long, thick, black hair that rested easily upon his broad shoulders, I raised my eyebrows and smiled nervously.

"I'm scared out of my freaking mind Dominik. I truly don't know that I want to give birth since I have no idea what to expect."

He moved gracefully like a wild animal to the side of the bed and sat down engulfing my smaller hands within his.

"You have no choice my sweet Jennalee. Tonight you will give birth to our child and we will become mates. It was forever meant to be and I have waited a long time."

I sat up quickly even though it hurt like hell to do so. "Tonight?" I exclaimed loudly, yanking my hands free of his grip. "Here in this bedroom...alone? Are you crazy, insane? No, don't answer that, I know the answer. You've called me that before so why was I selected?"

"You were chosen because of who your parents were and the lineage you come from. Plus, you won't be alone for I'll be here with you every second."

"I never knew my parents so how is this possible?" I inquired, suddenly wincing in severe pain, squeezing his fingers tightly.

"Your father was like me, a wolf, and your mother was human. It's the way of our race, how we continue to survive. Upon birth, your destiny was immediately intertwined with mine."

I suddenly screamed in agony, throwing my head back into the pillows. He moved closer and held me tight, letting my pain be absorbed by his own body.

Through clenched teeth, I moaned, "Then why did my parents abandon me? I was raised in terrible, disgusting foster homes until my last one when I was twelve."

"Your mother sadly died at your birth and your father was slain in a fight defending your honor and future existence. You then needed to be raised in a family environment as human as we could find. I'm sorry that it took several attempts to find Louise and Mark, but trust me my dear, those prior foster parents were taken care of."

"I don't even want to know what that means," before a loud yelp escaped my lungs, the pain seeming to split my body apart.

He pushed me gently backwards and stared into my eyes. "Your mother died of internal complications that will not happen to you. It cannot happen again, but you are different than she was, much stronger."

The pain was so intense at this point that any intelligible words were not possible, but I managed to ask, "Who killed my father?"

After a slight hesitation, he responded, "I did."

Once again I screamed into the night and yelled out, "I hate you."

Arching my back, I spread my legs and waited for the inevitable. Along with the physical pain was the mental torment over realizing that I had more than likely killed my own mother.

Since it felt like I was also being torn apart from the inside out, I lost conscience feeling that I was about to die just like she had.

Sometime later with no idea how much time had actually passed, I opened my eyes. The room was quiet and dark with only a small lamp glowing on the nightstand. I sensed movement to my left before Dominik appeared. He held something tiny that squirmed inside a warm, thick blanket.

"How are you Jennalee? Everything went fine and you will survive, believe me."

I stared at his face, not sure if I loved or hated him, a creature who was not only the killer of my father, but the reason for this nightmare I was now so lost within. The squirming inside the blanket stopped as if it sensed being near me.

"What are you holding?" I asked warily, as if I didn't already know.

He smiled warmly like any proud father would. "This is our child, your son. Would you like to hold him? I think he definitely wants his mother."

"No, please take it away."

"Jenna, he needs you. We need you."

I stared at his wildly handsome features, the pleading look in his eyes, the blanket containing something I had given birth to.

"Fine, then hand him to me."

Dominik bent down and placed the blanket containing the baby on my stomach and breasts. It stirred with noticeable excitement now lying upon his mother. Perhaps he was hungry I thought.

Reaching for the blanket, I placed one hand on top and let the other one slide beneath the material. I immediately froze as the baby moved. My fingertips touched fur as small teeth and sharp claws clutched hold of my hand.

The bedroom began to swirl and spin as I passed out, my last conscious thought being that I had just given birth to a damn puppy, a wolf cub. Perhaps I was not human after all.

THE END

FOREVER LOVE TRILOGY

(This is my own version and poetic slant on Sleeping Beauty)

A KISS BITTER SWEET

Part I

My Prince, you whisper to me in shadows.
You have appeared to me in mist.
Will this sleep of dreams be at an end?
How these urgent lips await your anxious kiss.

Dear sweet love of frenzied passion,
my pure paragon of desire,
please hold me tight within your arms
to soar away upon wings of perfect rapture.

I nervously sense you here beside me
and can hear thy heartbeat matching mine.
My prayers to you now spring alive
as lips unite, sweet kiss divine.

Wild hearts now set afire, my eyes aflutter,
I see your smiling eyes above me.
Sweet paramour thou' come to fulfill my dreams,
to hold me close, how much I've long to meet thee.

Yet, I feel an abhorrent darkness hovering
as I hear your breath fade to such a tragic end.
My anguished tears drip sadly upon your face,
envisioning a loss I shan't ever comprehend.

B'neath black storm clouds from Darkando's wings
oozed a voice that rained down fears.
"Do you truly think my dear that a kiss of such desire
might ever release you from your prison of tears?"

"Tis' true, you may be awakened in one hundred years
by the amorous love and devotion of another.
Alas my little beauty, the kiss that set you free came far too late,
your last breath stolen from your ill-fated lover."

Amidst the cackling laugh of Brucella, a tarnished,
silver goblet appeared beside a blood-red rose.
"You have but three choices my fair-haired beauty, for how
you choose only your tortured heart shall know."
"Stay awake to live and know your kiss thus slew your Prince.
Prick your finger upon the rose's thorn and sleep once more.
Sip from the goblet and unite with your lover forever.
So now my Beauty, is your dream of love worth dying for?"

The wicked voice echoed under rolling thunder
as the evil fairy and her diabolic raven flew away.
A brilliant sun appeared to bathe us in passionate afterglow.
"Oh sweet Prince, without you near there shan't be smiling days."

My shaking fingers clutched the poisoned chalice,
fully aware our love surpassed all that death shall now portend.
Very slowly I allowed my fate to touch a quivering mouth,
thus forever uniting our love to bring this nightmare to an end.

A SLEEP OF DREAMS

Part II

Tis' quiet ~ ~ so deathly quiet.
The gentle warble of a courting sparrow
flows serenely above the soft gurgle
of a stream amid tranquil flow.
Gentle breezes whistle through the treetops
eagerly whispering your name ~~
sweet key to thy broken heart.

Oh my beloved, where art thou?
I continue to slowly drift
in silent loneliness, awaiting
the firm press of your lips
to arouse me and awaken my desire,
to unlock this magical spell
to whence I've slipped.

Lost amid my fading dreams
I see you within the mist and reach desperately
to caress your smile, to touch
the gleam from your eyes, and let
my yearning fingertips trace
the contours of your face.
Oh, please awaken me.

I so beseech thee!
My tears moan through this evil
darkness cast upon me by Brucella, spread
o'er top like a shroud from Darkando's wings.
Endorra and Eelanna whisper Shandorra,
as Keriether cries out to her smiling rose.
I weep ~~ for I know not who they call to.

Forever lost, I continue to sleep.
A repose of angels ~ sad dream of sorrow.
Prescient dreams evolving into nightmares, sweet love
evaporating to dust, tears racing frantically
upon dark, raging dreams of no return.
Silently I await your kiss, locked
away in my reticent nocturne.

UNBROKEN LOVE

Part III

It felt like I was gently flying, with the bitter
taste of hemlock still brushed upon my lips.
Our names were being whispered on sighs throughout
the sobbing woods, happiness found for but a fleeting moment
before a spurned and hateful fairy cast our love upon the winds.
An angry storm of tragedy that had me calling out,
"My Prince of Hearts, where art thou?"
From the brink of Heaven's door I heard a whisper.

"I am here my love,"
came your firm and gentle voice.
"Reach out for me and grasp my trembling hand so we
may spend eternity together, our hearts as one at last."
I extended my hand and felt your warm fingertips brush
against mine, a feeling sweet heavenly divine.

These eyes fluttered open and there you were,
my Prince of Passion, the man who set me free
so that upon my kiss your fate was sealed with
mine ~~ forever more.

Your fingertip wiped a tear from my eye
and then enwrapped me in your strong embrace.
Oh Lord, thank heaven my sleep of dreams
this time will be where angels gently soar.
I wistfully gazed at your handsome face
and whispered softly against your beating chest,
"I love you so."

Suddenly a screech, he had no chance to answer,
I felt myself falling, reeling backwards,
still desperately holding onto him, afraid to let go,
screaming atop the swirling winds,
"Don't release me my love."

Propelled into darkness and light, flashing broken
shadows spinning past my frightened eyes,
we found ourselves lying on firm ground,
completely encircled in a massive, glowing bubble.
Shrill cries of agitated fairies chanting,

"Double bubble, toil and trouble,
break this spell of poisoned kisses.
Grumble, mumble, boil, and stubble,
return to us our Prince and Princess."

With a loud POP, POP, POP the bubble burst,
spilling us at the feet of Keriether who danced in glee.
A grinning Endorra and Eelanna, with great flourish,
stashed away their magic dust of roses and ambergris.
My arms still tightly holding onto my Prince
I smiled fondly into his eyes,
"Is this real my love, are we alive?"
"Yes, yes, yes pretty Princess," jabbered Endorra.
"Do you think we would let our Rich'arde and Shandorra
be taken from us by a fallen, nasty fairy?"

I smiled and twirled to face my Prince.
"Please take me in your arms to never let me go.
My enchanted heart is yours forever, never
to spend another moment without thinking of you.
Let my kisses now enrapture, let our hearts
be thus enamored, let this spell of love
and passion be our life's ambition."
Then he swept me in his arms,
unafraid to kiss me once again.
"I am yours from now until forever,"
he proclaimed for all the world to hear.
"My sweet love for you will
never, ever end."

KATIE, SPOTS AND ALL

Written in memory for one of the sweetest, most lovable dogs ever.

The tiny Dalmatian cocked her cute little head
in that sweet, curious way that puppies do.
"I'll just show them my best smile," she slyly thought.
"Hey, here I am! Over here! Right down here! Yoohoo!"
Oh no, she realized, they're not going to pick me.
Her smile now faded, eyes downcast, so distraught!

Suddenly she hears the door open and gazes up with hope.
Oh boy, Oh boy, Oh boy, they're coming back.
She wags her tail and prances around, for she's no dope.
"Yes, you just know you should've taken me,
but I won't hold that against you.
You'll be so happy, wait and see. My name is Katie!"

Months race by and like a wild hair, I continue to grow.
I'm tall and strong, just littered with black spots.
Oh my, Mommy's so mad though, and she scolds a lot.
I'm just a puppy, but I've been so bad, I know.
I realize she loves me and pray they don't take me back,
because this is my home and I love them so.

A few years coast by. Guess what? Yep, I'm still here!
"Hey Daddy, come on, come on, let's have some fun
and I'll take you out for a walk," she cries.
"That's right, get my leash, hook it on, have no fear."
"Weeee, let's go Daddy, see spot run," as she flies
by the window, Daddy in tow, hanging on for dear life.

So time has crept by and I'm now in my senior years.
I have slowed down a bit, I must admit.
When I think back I know it's been a good life.
Mommy and Daddy have loved and taken good care of me.
As I curl up in my bed beneath a soft, cozy blanket
I smile and sigh with happiness for it's no time for tears.

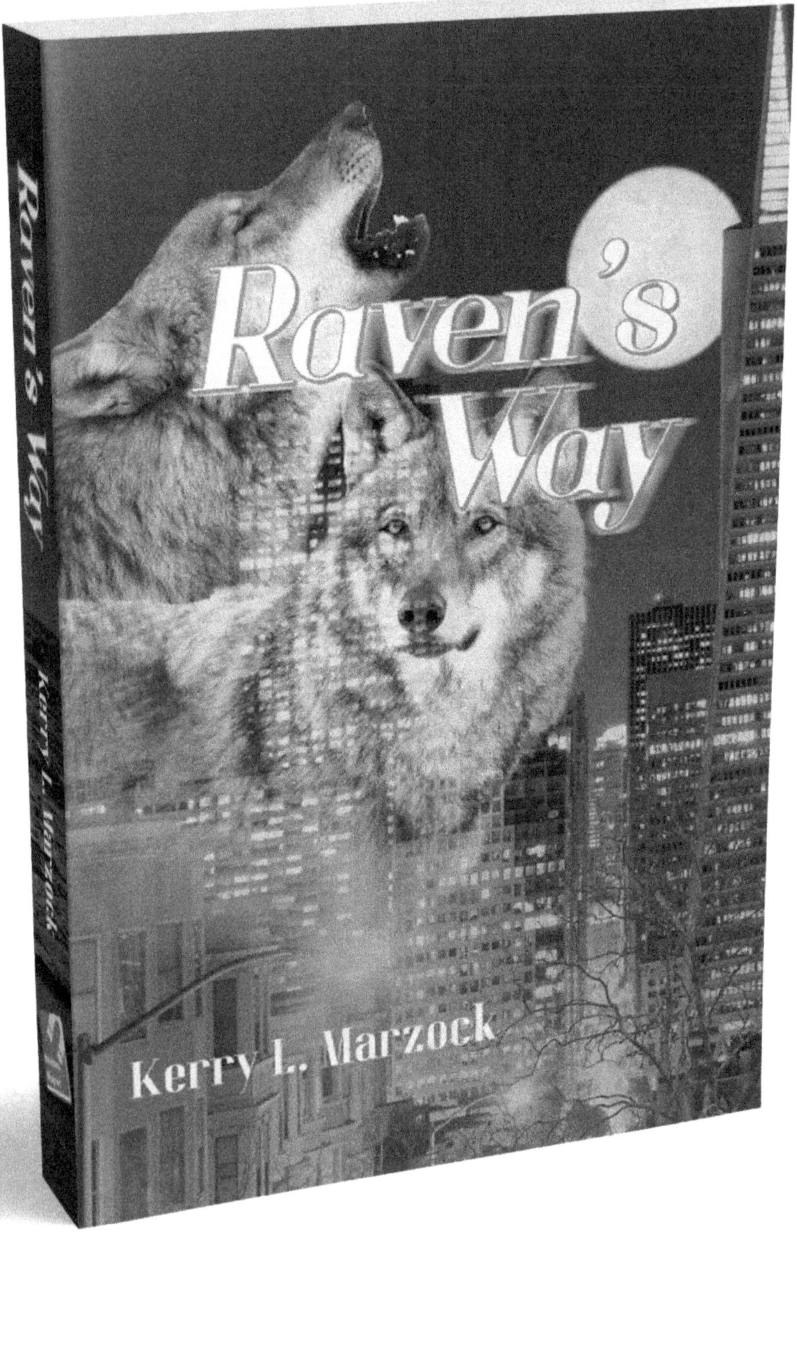
Raven's Way
Kerry L. Marzock
Raven's Way
Kerry L. Marzock

Raven's Way

Chapter 1

There was death in the air. Pure evil! Other than the occasional nervous chirp of an anxious cricket, the loudest sound in the restless air was the wayward call of a lonely owl echoing off the bleak darkness. A silky whisper of brittle leaves warily danced across the forest carpet, adding a peculiar spookiness to this scene ripped from the pages of any first-rate horror novel. However, this was real and hell was near.

It was obscenely quiet! Danger grabbed the night in a strangle hold of ominous ferocity. Animals that normally romped by day now huddled shivering in their tiny dens this very night, and not from the bite of winter winds, but rather the heart-stopping scent of death within their midst. Creatures that usually hunted underneath the veil of darkness knew enough to stay safe and not to venture out for fear they would become prey themselves.

And so the deadly quiet persisted!

Moonlight slithered through small cracks in the sheltering canopy above this quivering world. Sporadically, a piece of moonbeam would reflect off two feral, yellow ovals—eyes of the beast. It could easily be said this was not just any beast. The creature that stared with unblinking gaze was beyond the ken of human thought. Legends had been created about monsters that prowled underneath a full moon. Frightening tales whispered around flickering camp-fires, nightmares for those who believed in them, sheer terror for those who did not. For these nightmares to become reality then death would surely ensue. There were no enemies this insidious creature had to fear for he and his kind were the ones to be frightened of. Its world was the underbelly of humanity. His prey; those foolish enough not to believe in monsters and the cast-offs that society had all but rejected.

But under tonight's moonlit spell, this obscene creature itself was the prey. Harried voices broke the nighttime stillness, mingled with the frenzied baying of scent hounds whose bravery alone came from the manic urges of the pack and that of a firm master's hand. Scathing beams of flashlights, like an army of drunken Cyclops, sliced through the haunting, inky darkness. This frightened search party sought an unknown killer with a sickening picture of the mangled bodies of two young boys still etched horrifically upon their minds. Their slaughtered innocence had been discovered by a startled jogger in Fairmount Park beneath a sobbing moon. The beast they searched for was a destroyer of unspeakable savagery whose killing fields lay below a shivering heaven. Sadly, these brave men truly had no conception of what horror lay in wait for them, only the stark realization they could be slaughtered next.

A low rumble erupted from the beast's massive chest, enough to cripple with fear the staunchest of men. And, if someone was unlucky enough to hear this menacing growl, it would most likely be the next to last sound they heard before listening to the snapping of their own bones amidst a final death rattle.

The creature suddenly moved and slid like a mysterious shadow into the swirling fog. Death had now entered the arena and there was not a prayer to be spoken that would prevent it from happening. No weapon in their puny arsenal or faith and belief in a higher power, could help them this night. Blood would be shed because they dared search for a creature from their darkest nightmares.

In a spastic eruption, the dogs suddenly went berserk as they were assailed with the scent of a most dangerous prey. Quickly, barks of anxiety became cowardly whimpers and yelps of terror. Two frightened beagles broke free from their long tethers and sped off, hoping to see another sunrise, their master yelling obscenities and threats, but to no avail. Tango, a very misguided coon dog surged forward though, either extremely brave, or just too stupid to realize what lay in store for him. His older brother Charlie just stood his ground and growled a tepid warning, tail no longer wagging as nervous slobber dribbled from his quivering jowls.

Tango rushed forward and charged into the brush, anxious to please his handler and claim bragging rights. He stopped quickly, nose pointed to the ground, nostrils flaring as he picked up a scent never encountered before. But deep down, passed on through generations of hunting dogs before him, his brain registered danger while his fear screamed wolf.

With his frantic barks and mournful baying now ceased, the stillness was even thicker than before. Lonely crickets no longer chirped. Wary, observant owls were too alarmed to hoot a warning from their lonely lookout posts. Frightened dogs had completely lost any desire for the hunt.

Well, all but for that crazy Tango.

"Tango, Tango, hey boy," his handler yelled, followed by a sharp whistle. "You crazy coon dog, whatcha' got boy?"

Tango knew he had possibly heard the voice of his owner for the last time as he raised his head and stared at two bright yellow, murderous eyes. The coon dog's head dropped low as he curled his tail securely between his legs, falling to the ground in what he hoped would be a life-saving sign of submission.

It didn't work! The dark shadow with the ferocious glare moved at breathtaking speed. With a mighty swipe of massive claws, the monster severed the coon dogs head, sending it sailing through the moonlight like a spinning football heading for a game winning field goal. It landed no more than three feet in front of Nestor, Tango's handler, and then rolled awkwardly to lie at the quivering toes of a frightened Charlie.

"Holy shit!" Nestor screamed out loud, both in shock and rage. "OH my God, Tango. It killed my Tango."

A roar of unspeakable horror split the night, sending icy shivers up and down the spine of every policeman. Nestor couldn't pull his eyes away from the severed head of his beloved Tango. He felt his arm yank up and back, his hand releasing the other leash. Charlie knew enough to turn and tear ass from whatever creature was out there. Nestor, however, was not that smart.

Hearing another roar and then a wild thrashing of brush, he glanced up and came face-to-face with a heart-stopping vision of evil. A mouth full of slavering fangs and fetid breath was no more than six inches away from his very frightened face, the beast staring at him with maniacal hatred and a monstrous need to kill.

Nestor, with warm urine pouring down his pant leg, had but a few seconds to whisper "Dear God, forgive me for I have sinned ...." before his throat was savagely torn out and death viciously yanked him away.

Suddenly, the night erupted with frenzied shouts of nervous policemen, followed by a rapid volley of panicky gunfire. Flashes from urgent rifles lit for a second the terrified eyes of each shooter. Bullets whizzed and crashed against innocent trees, with an occasional scream of pain when one impacted soft, human flesh, jellied from fear.

"Hold your fire! Damn it, stop shooting," yelled a frenetic voice.

Echoes repeatedly bounced around like a soccer ball as Captain Ganz tried desperately to minimize the damage from friendly fire being inflicted by his own men. As the crescendo died down the only sounds Ganz heard were the rapid breathing of Officer Leightman to his left and the unsteady pounding of his own slightly damaged heart. He figured this was not good therapy for the newly inserted stents that now resided in two of his arteries. Suddenly, he was startled as a frightened coon dog nearly bowled him over, Charlie racing by to follow the paw prints of his deserting beagle brethren.

"Nestor, hey Nestor, you okay? Can anybody out there see where Nestor is?"

Getting no response from his good friend was not the answer Ganz had hoped to receive. Then he heard a startled voice and glanced to his right.

"Captain, over here... holy shit," followed immediately by loud, rapid heaves resulting in the violent eruption of an earlier dinner of chicken pot pie and mashed taters.

Ganz grabbed Leightman by the shoulder and, after pushing the officer's rifle away from his own face, moved towards the direction of where the vomiting was still coming from. He thought this night was just becoming more and more of a nightmare. What kind of unspeakable hell were they stalking? Lord, for that matter, what now monstrously hunted them?

He felt Leightman stumble and fall forward. Ganz immediately swerved and pointed his flashlight toward the ground. Quickly, the cheeseburger and fries he had eaten around seven o' clock almost roared back up his throat.

Leightman lay sprawled across Nestor's savaged body, his flashlight beam shining garishly upon dark blood still spurting wildly from two evenly severed carotid arteries. Off to the right, with tongue lolling from the side of an open mouth, stared the black, unseeing eyes of Tango. Ganz felt himself reeling backwards before he was held up by someone closely behind him.

"Jesus H. Christ, what did this? What kind of monster is out there?" whispered Captain Nathan Ganz. He had spent nearly thirty years on the Philadelphia police force and had never in his entire career been this terrified of anything in his life. But he clearly knew that what they now faced was not taught in any classroom at the academy, or faced on any street corner with some gun-wielding assailant. Monsters like this were not ever meant to exist outside of nightmares and movie screens.

With a silver moon glittering off the tranquil, black water of a peacefully meandering Schuylkill River the distinct, savage howl of a rapacious wolf vibrated the stark Philadelphia skyline. Captain Ganz instinctively made the sign of a cross as he stared down at the mutilated body of Nestor Shirreck and the head of his beloved Tango.

Thank God tomorrow was Sunday because he desperately needed to talk this one over with the big guy upstairs, along with Father Joseph who thought Nathan was a little crazy anyway. Especially since wolves, or monsters, were not supposed to exist in his wonderful City of Brotherly Love.

RAVEN'S RAGE
KERRY L. MARZOCK
RAVEN'S RAGE
ORDER OF THE CLAW
KERRY L. MARZOCK

Raven's Rage

Chapter 1

This evening was one of those bitterly cold, late January nights. It was the kind of steel-blade cold that can nastily grab hold of your body like an evil hand clutching your shivering bones with monstrous intent. Puffs of white steam exploded from the horse's quivering nostrils like an old time steam locomotive crawling up the tracks of a long hill, coughing out painfully "I think I can, I think I can..." The steady clip-clop of hooves on the lonely pavement echoed with intense apprehension. Accompanied by a nervous whinny now and then, the horse's acute senses were on high alert for some-thing dangerous, possibly deadly. The animal was simply not aware of why, or for what terrible reason. It somehow sensed that death was out there in the darkness waiting to strike violently from some unsuspecting direction.

Inside the small, one-seat buggy rode Adam Yost and Hannah Klinefelter. They tightly clutched frigid hands, a thick woolen blanket covering their legs. Even though quite tired, they were still beaming over the wonderful day spent at their closest friend's wedding. The adoration this young Amish couple had for each other was strengthened even more after seeing the happiness of new-found wedding bliss displayed by their longtime friends, Jacob and Abigail Neff. Their special moment could not happen soon enough. Hannah was already planning the loving dinner she would prepare on some future Sunday for Adam. At that time, they would announce their plans of marriage when their parents returned from the normal Sunday gathering of families. It was traditional for the Amish, 'plain folk' as they call themselves, to make their intentions known in this fashion and then have it broadcast to the entire community during church services. They had talked in hushed tones all throughout the day, giggling and whispering their own versions of sweet nothings. Proud parents gazed at them with fondness, aware that sometime in the near future their children would be starting a family of their own.

Hannah squeezed Adam's hand and smiled lovingly. She stared up into his strong, yet soft and dreamy, brown eyes with feelings she had never experienced for anybody else. He was a wonderfully considerate man from a proper, well respected family. It seemed as if they had been together already most of their lives, meeting each other as young children in school and spending a number of amorous, exciting moments in the barn hidden amid dark shadows in the hayloft. Hannah had been courted by a handful of other boys her age, but none ever compared to Adam, tall with a strongly chiseled face, compassionate and so concerned for her happiness. He would be a deeply devoted, honorable husband and such a loving, thoughtful father.

Adam leaned down and kissed her lightly on the forehead. He stared into her sky-blue eyes that sparkled in the light of passing street lamps, doll-like porcelain skin shining with just a touch of crimson on her cheeks. In one way it was from the January cold, but mostly from the love she felt for Adam. He knew, and rightly so, that he was without a doubt the luckiest young man in their surrounding Amish community, though at the moment he realized he shared that right with his best friend Jacob. His lucky friend would soon be spending that first nervous night with the woman he had just wed. "I wonderful luff you," Adam whispered softly, his lips brushing hers.

Excitement streaked through her body as she murmured back, "You're my Adam, I luff you so much too," her heart beating madly with the feelings she held for him.

Staring at the long expanse of empty road, he clucked a few times to his seemingly nervous horse. Gently snapping the reins, he felt a razor sharp edge of concern. It was darker than normal since the new moon cast off no light making those areas between street lamps relatively dark. A new moon occurs when the sun, earth, and moon are all in alignment, with the moon positioned between earth and the sun. As a result, the moon cannot be seen on these nights, unless there happens to be an eclipse. And for many, the new moon beckons a time of rebirth, especially monsters. Thus, Adam was thankful for the glowing street lamps along this lonely stretch of Route 322.

He also noted how sparse traffic was and then realized it was in fact bordering upon the stroke of midnight. Both of them had decided to spend a little more time with Jacob and Abigail in order to reveal their own plans for the coming year. He knew their parents would be extremely worried that the young couple had stayed out so late. They would be scolded upon their return home and would have to promise they would never be so inconsiderate in the future.

Yet feeling warmly aglow deep inside, he was also aware of a very evident nervousness in his horse.

A very trusting animal, he had painstakingly raised the spirited foal with loving care and patient tutoring, always his normal course of action. It took a long while preparing a horse to become fearless enough to pull rickety buggies and trot along these busy, congested roadways. They had to get used to being passed constantly by roaring trucks, diesel-smelling buses, and honking, inconsiderate drivers who seemed far too damn impatient to get nowhere fast. Unfortunately, all roads in the area had claimed lives, Amish as well as their horses. The shoulders and road-side fields were scarred with shattered debris from splintered carriages due to careless and stupid drivers.

Tonight would be no exception. Death now hovered mere seconds away. It would not come from a careless driver either, but rather an evil which Adam or Hannah could never have come close to imagining in their wildest nightmares.

The horse suddenly shied to the left with a frantic snort of fear, veering away from a dense thicket of brush off the road to the right. Adam frantically tugged hard on the reins, trying to calm down the frightened horse with a few sharp whistles. Silly really, as if a whistle could abate the panic now nearly paralyzing the crazed animal.

"Adam, vas is los?" cried out Hannah, clutching his arm in alarm with both hands.

Adam, however, was much too concerned in attempting to control the horse and keep them from tipping over. He was just grateful there was no oncoming traffic to avoid. It was not a vehicle he had to be alarmed about though as a huge shadowy form leaped from the bushes. A deafening roar tore the night apart. This nightmarish apparition struck the frightened horse with the force of a tractor trailer, raking the screaming animal's neck open as easily as a hunter slices into the underbelly of a slaughtered deer.

The horse was dead before hitting the ground with a nearly severed head lying at a most unnatural angle. The momentum of the attack spun the buggy around in a violent, hair-raising slide on two wheels. Tipping over completely, it broke free from the dead horse and then tumbled several times in a dizzying, grinding crash. Black pieces of wood and shards of glass were flung in an exploding shower of debris.

As was Adam's body, striking the ground with a loud, sickening thump, arms and legs bent at angles only meant for a Raggedy-Ann doll. His damaged body slid across the pavement where it violently struck the post of a road sign that claimed 'No Passing'. Even then, his only thought was for Hannah's safety. He peered through a reddish haze of blood streaming from a horrible, ugly gash across his forehead, searching frantically for the woman he loved.

The buggy laid upside down, crushed and broken, wheels spinning like a carnival ride in the chilly, midnight air. Hannah's stunned and broken body was securely pinned underneath a pile of debris. Her screams still echoed across the empty fields, praying that somebody would hear their plea before she and her beloved Adam were dead. Surprisingly, she was still semi-conscious, though gripped in terrible, agonizing pain from a fractured leg and a broken back. She could see the horse lying crumpled on the pavement, two legs reaching up towards the nighttime sky in silent supplication. It's nearly severed head was surrounded by a pool of blood appearing like a dark, jet-black pond of hematite beneath a streetlamp's severe glare.

Another terrifying roar violently shook the night as Hannah let her frightened gaze peer through several openings in the destroyed buggy surrounding her. Suddenly, through one of the larger holes, a menacing shadow slithered across a thin shaft of light. She prayed it was a passing motorist who had thankfully stopped to give assistance. Sadly though, prayers aren't always answered.

"Help me please, I beg thee," she croaked, unable to move, surprised that the initial pain was now succumbing to a grateful blanket of numbness.

But lifesaving assistance was nowhere near, only a violent death the young, innocent Amish couple could never have imagined. Suddenly she felt the buggy being angrily lifted, dumping her to the pavement in a broken heap. Her pretty head struck the ground in a sickening thump like an overripe apple falling from a tree. Thankfully though, her beseeching prayers of assistance went unanswered since she would be unable to realize the nightmarish evil that had befallen them. The concussion was such that she gratefully did not notice the long, hairy feet which had moved up to straddle her body. Even though she was still somewhat quasi-conscious, the ground and surrounding landscape had a surreal, alien feel. It felt like a dream, as if she was floating above the ground looking at the accident scene.

Adam numbly witnessed the entire, horrifying event through a nearly black, crimson curtain of blood that still flowed from his badly lacerated head, total surrender of life possibly minutes away. He was able to slowly slide his arm towards his beloved Hannah as she was lifted off the ground. She hung clutched in the massive claws of a devilish beast. Whispering her name for nobody to hear but himself, Adam watched in horror as the young Amish girl he dearly loved was lifted towards a nightmarish, wolfish head. Through eyes that were now barely open, he saw that monstrous mouth open to unveil huge, slobbering fangs, horrid teeth which no living creature should ever possess.

Before passing out Adam stared with a horrified gaze as the beast stuffed pretty Hannah's thin neck between vile, frightening jaws. The young Amish man felt anguish in that he could not protect his beloved. He prayed that death would sweep him away towards a darkness he hoped to never escape from. To go on living and remembering this night would be like existing in a living nightmare. Thankfully, Adam did not see the creature crawl towards the barren, empty field, dragging his beloved Hannah behind. Her dead feet bounced roughly across the skeletal remains of broken corn stalks, tattered long black skirt flapping in the icy breeze. Her blood-splattered bonnet lay alone upon the pavement. It was all that remained of her youthful existence.

Through the dense quiet which had quickly settled over the accident scene, a spine-tingling howl splintered the stillness. Lights in nearby farmhouses quickly blinked on. Adam fortunately did not hear the cry of the beast for he seemed demonically lost in the oblivion of his own ongoing nightmare. He not only had lost the woman he loved, but also the will to go on living. Before total darkness overtook him, he reached forward with bloody fingers and whispered, "Hannah, I love thee... please...forgive...."

www.ingramcontent.com/pod-product-compliance
Lightning Source LLC
LaVergne TN
LVHW021047100526
838202LV00079B/4698